T0106845

San Casimiro, TEXAS

SHORT STORIES

Mario E. Martinez

authorHOUSE®

AuthorHouse™
1663 Liberty Drive
Bloomington, IN 47403
www.authorhouse.com
Phone: 1-800-839-8640

© 2012. Mario E. Martinez. All Rights Reserved.

No part of this book may be reproduced, stored in a retrieval system, or transmitted by any means without the written permission of the author.

Published by AuthorHouse   12/6/2012

ISBN: 978-1-4772-9262-4 (sc)
ISBN: 978-1-4772-9261-7 (hc)
ISBN: 978-1-4772-9260-0 (e)

Library of Congress Control Number: 2012921830

Any people depicted in stock imagery provided by Thinkstock are models, and such images are being used for illustrative purposes only. Certain stock imagery © Thinkstock.

This book is printed on acid-free paper.

Because of the dynamic nature of the Internet, any web addresses or links contained in this book may have changed since publication and may no longer be valid. The views expressed in this work are solely those of the author and do not necessarily reflect the views of the publisher, and the publisher hereby disclaims any responsibility for them.

Other Works by Mario E. Martinez

Twin Burials

This book is dedicated to

Erica Vela

with whose help these stories wouldn't be possible.

She was there when I first laid the foundations of San Casimiro, Texas

and she will be there when I burn it down.

The author would like to thank Luz M. González-
Espino for all her help with this collection.

One objection I have heard voiced to works of this kind—dealing with Texas—is the amount of gore spilled across the pages. It can not be otherwise. In order to write a realistic and true history of any part of the Southwest, one must narrate such things, even at the risk of monotony.

—Robert E. Howard

The town had, of course, always displayed certain peculiar and often profoundly surprising qualities and features. Sooner or later everyone who was a permanent resident there was confronted with something of a nearly insupportable oddity or corruption.

—Thomas Ligotti
"In a Foreign Town, In a Foreign Land"

Contents

A Little Friendly Competition

I.

Nadine Peckings had the house clean for her husband's arrival. Their son, Elias Jr., was outside playing with a stick, chasing the sparrows out of the bushes. She pushed her auburn hair from her face and scanned the front room and dining room. Everything was satisfactory. She watched the clock from the couch, waiting to hear the rumbling of her husband's truck and trailer. He'd spent the day at the Refugio Farmer's Market, where vendors from three counties gathered to sell their homemade preserves and cakes, their odd birdhouses and marmalades.

Elias sold none of those things. He was a mortician by trade, and Elias Peckings' Funeral Services had the market cornered in Refugio and most of San Casimiro. But, on the day of the Farmer's Market, Elias threw off his mantle of mortician, cleaner of the dead, and took on another. He'd made hamburgers and ribs for the past six years, a staple in lot eight at the end of the market grounds. For Elias, it was the day people could look him in the eye without malice or anger. He often saw most of the area's residents at work, but there, understandably, they were not the friendliest. A lover, a son, a father, had passed, and no amount of good wishes on Elias's part could break the moods his business seemed to exude.

But, filling the market grounds with the smell of charred beef and fresh cut vegetables, people laughed with him, looked him in his rather odd face. One eye seemed on the verge of shutting while the other was open and vibrant. They'd stand and converse with him about mundane topics, but they were conversations not interrupted by tears. Selling burgers, Elias felt like he was a member of the community, someone not just kept around because of a sad need, a dire reality, but because there was something he could do that could bring joy instead of misery, instead of a dignity in death.

Nadine thought about the smiling face Elias wore every year when he walked through their front door. She thought about it so hard she wondered if the sounds of his truck and trailer were merely something in her own imagination, but a moment later, she knew it wasn't.

Elias pulled into the driveway, dragging a large trailer converted to house three grilling units complete with charcoal pits and compartments for seasonings and condiments. Nadine looked out the window and smiled as the truck door opened, but something was different. When Elias put his foot on the ground, it looked as though it weighed an astronomical amount, as though the mere movement of the appendage were a trial Elias had to endure. When she caught sight of his face, Nadine's hand crept up toward her mouth. True, one of Elias's eyes was incapable of opening fully to reveal anything, but the other eye was just as closed. No smile could be traced along the edges of his mouth, just a deep scowl and distant look of contemplation.

He moved up the driveway slowly, not even bothering to retrieve any remaining food from the truck. He was a thin man of light skin with longish hair circling his balding head like a Chaucerian monk.

Nadine opened the door for him, asking, "How'd it go, honey?" Her smile was forced, but she thought it the only thing she could do.

Elias didn't immediately answer, only walked past her and into the living room. A thick aroma of smoke and cooked beef followed him. He collapsed on the couch and pushed back his head with both his hands. He sat like that for a moment, silent and stretching.

"Is something the matter, dear?" Nadine asked.

"Where's Eli?" Elias asked through his hands.

"He's playing outside," Nadine said.

"Good," Elias said slowly. Then, he screeched into his hands. The note was shrill and lasted longer than Nadine would've preferred. She's seen the pose before, heard the moan of anguish in her husband's voice, but usually, it was after a busy day at the mortuary. The last time she'd seen him so flustered was when the Miller family lost control of their sedan and all four of them were killed in the roll-over crash. Elias had to work two days to have the bodies ready to be viewed and buried. But, the mortuary was closed that day on account of the Farmer's Market. As far as she knew, no one had died.

"Elias, what happened?" Nadine asked.

Elias dropped his hands to his sides, but left his head tilted back so that he could fully take in the popcorn ceiling. "Robert-god-damn-Fennerman is what happened, Nadine," he said and sighed. "I got there at eight, like I always do. My lot was ready for me, so I set up. The charcoal took a bit to get going. I mean, the whole market was already going by the time I got the fire ready. And, you've seen me sell those burgers. I've got people ready to claim the first one before I unwrap the patties. So, naturally, I thought it was weird that no one was there yet."

"Maybe they just saw you weren't ready," Nadine offered, thinking that was the trouble with her husband. He was normally a sensitive man, but even he knew the fickleness of customers, especially ones so removed from cities.

"That wasn't even it, Nadine," Elias went on. "I got the fire going, and I was so into making sure that I had everything going, that I didn't notice the smell of burgers."

"I thought you said you hadn't cooked them," Nadine said.

"I hadn't," Elias said and shook his head. "Fennerman was. He set up at lot twelve. He was making sliders. Little hamburgers with some onions and a little cheese. I saw those things, paper thin beef patties and stringy onions. But, I was at the end of the Market, so I got to watch him sell overpriced little burgers and buns the whole day. I'd be sold out by noon, usually. Now, I have to go to the shelter in Refugio to drop off what we've got left. That son of a bitch—"

"Elias!"

"It's true!" Elias shouted. "He knew I sold hamburgers every year at the market. People talked about it, Nadine. People would come up to me for a month and ask about those burgers. Today, I couldn't even sell half. By the time anyone got to me, they'd filled up on sliders and beer. I even asked the Willis kid to buy one for me so I could see what the fuss was about."

"How were they?" Nadine asked.

Elias didn't answer immediately, only stared forward as though remembering the bite. "Good. Not as good as mine, but good enough to mess up my burger stand."

"It'll be better next year," Nadine said.

"It has to be, Nadine," Elias said. "I've got a year to do it. There's got to be something that'll put my burgers back on top. I just have to find it."

"Well, don't worry honey," Nadine said and kissed his balding head. "A little friendly completion never hurt nobody."

II.

The thought of Robert Fennerman and his sliders infected Elias's mind the rest of that year. As he worked on the bodies of men and women, neighbors and acquaintances, that were carted into his funeral home, Elias smelled the grilled onions. He'd worked on so many corpses, seen his father before him work on so many, that most of the process was instinctual. He washed the bodies, draped modesty clothes over their dead genitals, and did the necessary tests his father had shown him. He worked the joints, moving them back and forth, making sure rigor mortis had set before he set at the task of working it out of the muscles. He then pulled the centrifugal pump and hose towards the work table. Afterward, it was just a matter of insertion and waiting. Insert the hose leading to the pump into the cadaver's neck. Once that was finished, inserted another hose across the corpse's neck to drain the old blood and body fluids. Without fail, Elias set the pump to work the mix of formaldehyde and other preservatives.

Once the process began, Elias thought of the Market and how to create a better burger, something so delicious no one would stop at Fennerman's stand. He pictured the sizzling meat, the thick smoke warming his skin, as he dressed the bodies in suits and hand-picked dresses. As he slid the mutli-pronged eye caps beneath the eyes of the deceased, Elias wondered if he should marinate the patties in a sauce or use the same dry-rub he'd used before. Massaging the forehead so the plastic eye covers could set naturally, creating the illusion of a peaceful slumber, Elias pretended he was rolling ground chuck into patties.

And, this was Elias's life for months. The bodies came out roughly dressed and only partially assuaged of their rigor mortis. At one funeral, one for a young man killed in a hunting accident, it seemed as though the corpse attempted to puff out its chest because its arms were too stiff to lie close to the body. At another, Elias only partially removed the innards, filling the viewing hall with the rank stench of preservatives and the faint smell of death. Even after some people complained about the state of their departed loved ones, Elias couldn't shake the constant thinking about the Farmer's Market, about Fennerman's sliders.

Soon, he was so consumed with the idea, that he brought a cheap hotplate into the preparation room so that he could experiment on the different ways to make a hamburger. As the embalming machine pumped synthetic preservatives into the corpses of the tri-county area, Elias hunched over his hotplate and skillet, working with patties formed from an 85/15 chuck ground up himself. He seasoned it with a bit more lemon zest, but the new flavor was hardly noticeable. He tried marinating the patties in Worchester sauce, but the sharp new taste wasn't enough. Yes, perhaps it would fool children into thinking the burgers were something to come running for, but they wouldn't be enough to beat Fennerman.

The answer came from one of Elias's best customers, Silvio Magaña, who died from a heart attack. Silvio was a large man, well over three hundred pounds of mostly fat and hair. Elias's father had taught him that with larger bodies, the embalming process could take twice as long. The arteries were usually so clogged that the thickened blood needed to be flushed slowly as to not pop any of the veins. Elias worked on Silvio as much as his wandering mind allowed him, but ultimately returned to thoughts of adding onions to his own burgers to enhance the flavor. He worked on two patties, one using his original technique, and another made with garlic powder and even less fat. He flipped both and watched them sizzle in their own grease, browning expertly.

Then, the sputtering began.

Elias turned in horror to see the pump flooding Silvio's veins with embalming fluid. From the drainage tube, the lumpy black blood splashed on the ground and whipped wildly, covering one wall with flecks of gore. Elias tried to get to the machine in time, but before he could shut it off completely, the drainage hose tore a hole into the side of Silvio's neck, releasing crumbles of congealed fat along with the blood. He stared at the torn neck and cursed himself. Elias knew the repair would take him most of the night to finish and the remainder to make it look like some mad experiment hadn't befallen Silvio. He sighed and listened to the sizzling burgers.

He returned to the hotplate and removed both patties. He bit into the one with garlic, but the spice overpowered the natural taste of the meat so much so that Elias simply threw it away. He bit into the other, awaiting the familiar taste of the burger he'd been selling for a decade. Yet, when he expected the same flavor to hit his tongue, it was flooded like Silvio's veins. Something was succulent about that burger where the others were simply reminders of his defeat at the hands of Fennerman. Something about that burger would have people passing lot twelve in order to line up in front of his burger stand. But, he couldn't tell what was different. He'd made it no different than any of the others. Formed it the same and spiced it the same. It was the consistency he'd used normally. Yet, there, next to the injured corpse of one of his best customers, Elias ate his burger as though it were the first one he'd ever tasted.

He knew the burger in his hands would be the one to lead him to victory, if only he knew why.

He noticed it once he cleaned the room. Silvio had been sewed up using a flesh colored thread and a suit jacket with a larger collar. Unless his wife thrashed the body around, no one would notice the puckered wound on the side of Silvio's neck. The mess was a considerable one, too. Blood had sprayed across one wall, contaminating a number of his clamps and scalpels. But, the worst was the congealed fat. He went over the room thoroughly, looking under tables and behind shelves, in order to find all the pieces. There were even some stuck on the ceiling, which he retrieved a ladder to clean. From that vantage point, with the fluorescent lights cascading down around him, he spotted another mark of fat hitting the walls.

Too his horror, the stain was above the hotplate.

He focused on the stain and moved down the ladder slowly, keeping it in sight. Elias stood next to Silvio's body and pointed at the wound with his finger. As though recreating the accident, Elias moved his finger to compensate for the drainage hose, then turned his finger, imagining the muck that flew as a result of the clogged veins. At one point, he completed a revolution with his finger and walked toward the hot plate, his finger tracing a trajectory in the air. He pressed his finger to the wall above the hotplate and found a small smudge, but no fat stuck to it. Then, he realized that the fat wouldn't have stuck to the wall in the first place. Silvio had been dead too long to keep the fat oily. By the time Silvio had been wheeled in, the fat had hardened to something like cottage cheese.

Elias looked at the spot and down at the hotplate, down over the spot where his burger had been. Part of him wanted to vomit, knowing what flavored the burger he knew could beat Fennerman, but another part simply thought and thought. For a moment, he almost considered it, the new flavoring. But, Elias put it out of his mind, knowing he couldn't do such a thing, Farmer's Market or not.

Two weeks before the Farmer's Market, Elias was at Rosita's, hoping to drown his anxieties with warm beer and cheap enchiladas. On the table across from him was a flyer, half dangling off the table, fluttering slightly with the circulating air tossed around by the ceiling fans. It would have passed his notice if he didn't see a large 'F' on the corner of it. He went and retrieved it before sitting back down at his table. Immediately, his hunger was gone. The flyer was for Fennerman's Sliders, to be sold at lot twelve in two weeks. They were quality flyers, colored and filled with pictures of glistening little burgers drooling American cheese.

Elias cursed his luck. He'd never even thought of advertising his burgers before, but, then again, there had never been a need to. Now, staring at Fennerman's flyer, Elias's hand shook as though truly realizing that failure lay a mere fourteen days away.

Once he returned to the mortuary, Elias couldn't fully concentrate on his work. The thought of Fennerman's sliders was too much for him. The name that he cultivated, the yearly ritual that made him less a social pariah and more so a pillar of the community, was slipping away. Soon, he'd just be another small town mortician, unloved by anyone other than his wife and son. No more were the days of sizzling meat and smiles shared under a summer sun. All that was left were the bodies on the tables, lifeless, to be cleaned and dressed for burial. He wondered if there was truly anything he could do, but there was nothing he could think of that didn't go back to Silvio's accident.

The thought lingered in his mind until the phone in the corner of the room rang. He picked it up, sullenly answering, "Peckings Funeral Home, this is Elias."

It was the sheriff. A collision occurred on the highway and three people were killed, all local.

"We're sending them over to you now, Elias," the sheriff told him. "And, you're going to have your work cut out for you, today. Ain't one of those people under two hundred and fifty pounds. Damn near gave the EMT a hernia just getting them on the gurneys."

Elias said he'd be ready for them and hung up. Again, he thought of the flyer. The small burgers that would run him out of the Farmer's Market. But, as he mulled over the images in his head, his eye caught hold of the bone scraper. A crude tool that was no more than a depressed trowel of stainless steel used to smooth out the lumps in the skin, to shear away any bits of organ that clung to the bones. He looked at it and thought of how easy it would be to collect fat with it, how easy it would be to take enough to cook with and sew the bodies up.

III.

The smell alone had a line forming around Elias's burger stand. There he stood, smiling with his monkish hair, his good eye glowing, while the other seemed relaxed. He flipped the burgers and smiled at the aromatic sizzle that came off them. From between the crowding bodies, Elias watched Fennerman desperately try to sell his sliders to every passing person, but they only held up their hands and indicated that they wanted whatever smelt so good.

Old Mrs. Tandy went up and ordered one from Elias, who smiled and said, "Coming right up, Betty." He placed the burger patty on a bun and dressed it properly.

"You've got quite the crowd today, Elias," Mrs. Tandy said. "I heard you've got some secret recipe you're trying this year."

"Oh, just a little of this and a little of that," Elias said and handed her the burger.

"Care to tell me what it is," Mrs. Tandy said as she handed Elias her money.

"Betty, I didn't even tell Nadine," Elias said. "Wouldn't even let her try one." He handed Mrs. Perkins her change and went on filling orders.

Mrs. Tandy waited until she was away from the crowd to take her first bite. The meat was juicy and flavorful, sending her taste buds into a tingling fit. Before she even realized it, she was halfway through with it. She looked so strange devouring her meal without a care for the world around her that Manuel, the town's general handy man since his work at the library culminated in a fire, had to call her name three times before she took notice. "Oh, Manuel," Mrs. Tandy said, giggling to herself. "You've got to eat one of Elias's burgers," she said. "I don't know what he did to make them different, but they're delicious."

"Well, he's had that stand for years," Manuel said. "I'm sure they're as good as last year."

"Even better," Mrs. Tandy exclaimed. "I swear, that Elias is one great cook."

"A man of many talents," Manuel said.

"Ain't that the truth," Mrs. Tandy agreed. "Got the county eating good one day, and taking care of the dead in the next. I swear, just last week, I sent my poor aunt, Milly, over to him."

"I was sorry to hear that," Manuel told her.

"Well, she was suffering," Mrs. Tandy said, not the least bit depressed at the thought of her aunt. The food was too good to let her spirits dampen. "But, I'll tell you, Elias made her look like a new woman in that coffin. I swear, she was skinnier in that coffin than she was in her whole life…My lord, this burger is good!"

—ETC.—

Nopalita

In the pre-dawn chill, the old man watched the caged cattle with his chin on his fist. Three men, yawning and smoking rolled cigarettes, stood behind the old man's perch on the fence in silence, the only sounds coming from the sharp puffs of breath blowing the ashes off their cheap tobacco. The Angus, black and lumbering in their cramped space, nursed calves and the two bulls, separated by a rusted gate, ate lazily. Inside the corral, the cows picked their heavy heads up from salt blocks, now only yellow-white debris, and bellowed their steaming breath to the morning. The old man grumbled to himself, summoning all eyes to him; it had been the first sound he made. "Ovidio," he said and the tallest of the three, nose furrowed and eyes squinted from the smoke rolling up to his wide-brimmed hat, stepped forward. "You and Pruneda push them from the back. Santiago, work the gate. Put them into this pen," he said and motioned to the one beside him, "and cut the calves."

All three nodded, stepped on their cigarettes, and dropped the butts into their front pockets or the lining of their hats. They scaled the short fences easily and walked through the muscular black sea that shifted nervously at their presence. As Ovidio and Pruneda moved towards the end of the corral, they picked up sturdy sticks from the ground; Santiago moved along the fence line to open the gate. The heavy thing swung easily, knocking against the fence and nearly sending the old man to the ground. He cursed at the short man, who could only reply, "Sorry, Mr. Brizuela, it got away from me."

"Be careless again and this job will get away from you!" Brizuela yelled. "Now, move, the lazy bunch of you! We've got work to do!"

With that, Ovidio let out a bark, slowly moving forward, netting the cows with the threat of his stick and harsh tones. The bovine moved in no rush, tearing themselves away from the salt scattered ground only when they noted the men's boots were too close for their liking. Once inside the next pen, Santiago slid the thick iron bolt into place, locking the cattle inside. The Angus crowded around the single tree partitioned off in the center of the pen. All three men stopped and looked at Brizuela who shot them annoyed glares and spurned them into action with a wave of his hand. He watched the workers without a word, flaring his wide nostrils as they walked into the holding pen and took their positions: Ovidio at the corner nearest to the old man, Pruneda in the thick of them, and Santiago at the gate.

With a yell and a crack of Pruneda's stick, the cattle started moving, their calves hiding about their legs. Once the cattle rounded the tree, spotting the open gate, they charged, losing their offspring in their dash, and when one of the black-brown calves tried to run through, the heavy gate slammed shut; the small creatures, sounding out for their mothers, went round the tree to join the rest. Like a carousel, the animals circled the sylvan pole, the cows granted passage to the salted corral and the calves, frightened and bawling, were locked inside.

At Brizuela's request, the three men moved to the furthest end of the quartered corral. Pruneda opened one gate and moved the bulls into the same pen and the others pushed the cows into the clear section of the corral easily, but still, the old man cursed them in two languages, pointing to the bulls. One lowered its head at the sight of the other and snorted. Both beasts charged, crashing head first into each other, and their hooves dug deep lines in the loose dirt until they disengaged. Ovidio and Santiago watched from the other side of the fence, and the tall man whispered, "Five bucks on the curly haired one."

The stout man considered it and agreed.

Brizuela was off his perch, waving his arms in the air, yelling, "*Pinches pendejos! Son of a bitch!*"

The two bulls charged again, and the curlier of the two toppled the other with a buck from its powerful neck. The other lost its feet and struck the fence behind it with its massive frame, breaking a hole into the aged planks before running off into the overgrown pasture.

"That's five," Ovidio chided.

"Ah, but we didn't shake on it," Santiago laughed and from across the corral, Pruneda nodded.

It was hot. The sun beat down on the clustered animals, and their black fur ate the heat like starved children, agitating their thick blood. The sounds of their calves, all pressed against the wooden fence with their snouts poking out drove them mad, and none of the men wanted to be behind them lest they be kicked. Yet, with Brizuela yelling in their ears from the broken corral, Santiago moved to the rear of the herd, and Ovidio stood on the thick metal pipes that made the funnel for the squeeze chute; at the jaws of the rusted flytrap, Pruneda sneezed from the dust moving in the corral like a fog.

One by one, the cows protested, but moved into the funnel in waves of four, and the lead dashed to exit only to be caught by the closing walls and guillotine door of the chute. The creatures shook the trap on its wooden beams, and Brizuela snatched the branding iron in the fire pit he'd set and plunged the sizzling metal onto the trapped haunches. Prudena hid his face from the thick acrid smoke as the slight breeze held it like a veil over his nose, and he could do nothing save hold his breath since both his hands held down the machine's lever.

"*Ándale!*" Brizuela yelled when he was satisfied with the mark. Once released, the animal charged out of the chute, falling amidst its own screams, warning the others of searing pain.

Soon, all the cattle had a familiar CB branded on them and Santiago laughed at the sight of it. "It looks like a buck-toothed smiley face," he told Ovidio who said it looked more like "a baby's ass peeking out of a onesie."

Brizuela lifted the brand out of the fire and poked the glowing rod at them, forcing them back a step. "CB! For Calixto Brizuela! Baby's ass," he shot at Santiago. "Let me brand you with it and see if you think it's like a baby's ass."

"Come on, boss. We're just joking around. Trying to pass the time," Ovidio said from his vantage point on the chute.

"My money should pass the time enough for you!" The old man's nostrils flared above his gray moustache as he scowled at all three of them. "Two days on the job and you're complaining that you're *bored*. Worthless! Ten years ago, you'd've been shot for being so useless." He threw his hands in the air. "Put out that fire and get in the truck, all of you!" he said and Pruneda kicked dirt onto the smoldering wood while Ovidio and Santiago followed Brizuela to his old white and green pick-up.

They drove past the lakes of buffel-grass, pale brown from the lack of rain, and Ovidio sat in the bouncing truck in silence, listening to Pruneda and Santiago laughing in the cluttered bed. "Don't stare off into nothing!" Brizuela said. "Look at the fences. One hole in them and I'm ruined. Old

Cazares would love to have his ugly Brahma's come in here and soil my crop. Nothing but loose skinned humps on those ugly animals. He'd be blessed to come out with a mess of Brangus."

"That's an ugly word," Ovidio accidentally said aloud.

"An ugly word for an ugly animal!" the old man fumed.

Brizuela slammed on the brakes, sending the two men in back flying forward into the truck's frame, and the vehicle skid to a stop. "My gun! My gun!" he pressed while his outstretched hand flapped in front of the ranch hand's face. Ovidio quickly handed him the old Winchester and Brizuela aimed off in the distance. The men peeked out of the truck, spotting a Harris hawk perched on a cactus blooming blood red flowers in the middle of a *caliche* pit. Brizuela shot, scaring the predatory bird away and forcing it to drop the half-torn rabbit it had been feasting on. Even though the bird was well into the sky, Brizuela cleared the empty shell and loaded another and another until he shot at nothing but a moving line in the on-going blue. "*Chinga!*" he spat as he jerked himself out of the dirty truck. Brizuela walked towards the lone tree cautiously as if waiting for some pit viper to burst out of the white dirt.

The three men followed. From the edge of the pit, they said nothing though the old man inspected the cactus closely. With his pocket knife, Brizuela skewered the remnants of the dead cottontail and walked to the rim of the granular circle. He tossed the partial corpse into the brush, nearly losing his knife in the process, before returning to them. "If any of you," he said waving his bloody knife at them to accentuate the point, "see something on that plant, you kill it. You see anything touch it, I want it dead! Understand?"

All the men exchanged odd glances, but shrugged and nodded without a word.

"I swear," he seethed, "if I come back next week and see so much as one *nopal* scratched, you'll wish I just fired you. Understand? I'll have the bunch of you shipped back to Mexico before you can say, 'Have mercy, *señor.*'"

"Sir," Ovidio interrupted. "I was born in El Paso."

"Try telling them that when I say you're a bunch of coke-mules and coyotes," the old man snapped back. Brizuela made his way back to the truck.

The workers followed.

Brizuela had been gone three days, and the work was not enough to fill up their time. The old cast iron grill was hot and ready with Pruneda only loosely watching it since his attention was on his prize, Panchita, the old Spanish guitar his grandfather had made by hand. He strummed it gently then tuned it with his ear close to the neck.

Ovidio reclined on a dusty rocking chair with his feet propped up on the firewood they hadn't used and he absently flipped through a dime store comic, giggling at the drawn women, always large breasted and too foolish to lock the door behind them; he wondered why the artists never thought to lock the door and let them get on with it. "Enough with your fiddle, Pruneda, it's killing me," he said.

"Leave him alone," said Santiago with a tray of fresh beef, bloody and hanging in lean ribbons. "I like it. And you're not doing anything. At least he's watching the fire. What are you doing, huh? Reading your dirty comics."

"I'm expanding my mind."

"Ah, you're expanding something," the stout man laughed and tossed the first slab of meat onto the grill. The butchered flesh cooked quickly and was eaten at the same speed. After he cleaned his fingers, Pruneda played an old song on his guitar. They all lounged, smoking their rolled cigarettes, but Santiago held a scowl and when asked what was the matter, he could only say, "I'm still hungry and I can't think of what the hell for," and turned his head towards Pruneda. "Anything left?"

"No, unless you want to lick the blood off the plates," he said.

"Not today, but…Ah!" Santiago spat as he stood. "I'm going to look for something. Who's coming with me?"

Ovidio nodded and followed Santiago to the old ranch truck; they both told Pruneda to clean. The ranch-hands drove along the dirt paths bordered with barbed wire wrapped onto gnarled wood and centered with metal T-posts. Neither spoke, only smoked and passed a small bottle of tequila between them. Ovidio tipped his head back, but Santiago suddenly broke, sending the stinging liquid all over his face. A curse started in his throat, but Santiago's exclamation cut it short: "That's the ticket!"

Ovidio looked out of the open window, spotting a large collection of cacti blooming yellow flowers on the green discs , but there was no way to reach it save braving the waist-high grass. "Good luck getting it," Ovidio laughed and Santiago raised his meaty hand to strike him, but lowered it with a laugh before shooting it out again and roughly disheveling Ovidio's coarse hair.

"That's the fun part," Santiago chided. "I've found what I wanted, and now I need to figure out how to get it. There are more cactuses—"

"Cacti," Ovidio corrected.

"Oh, the filthy reader is *so* smart," Santiago said and put the truck in gear.

They passed collections of the thorny plant, all vibrant green with their yellow blossoms glowing in the sun, but none had any path to them that didn't require a machete. "There has got to be one fucking patch of the—Aha!" he snapped and pressed his heavy foot on the gas. They flew down the road with a trail of thick dust behind them, and Ovidio gripped the window tightly as Santiago drove with a toothy grin and eyes possessed until halting near the *caliche* pit.

"What do you think you're doing?"

"I'm getting dessert, that's what."

"Brizuela told us—"

"That old fuck told us a lot of things. And I didn't hear a god damn one of them. Besides, who's going to notice two pears missing?"

"Brizuela."

"Ah, we'll just tell him it was one of his cows. We can't be watching that tree all day. You're not thinking of ratting me out are you?" Santiago asked.

"What for? I get paid the same whether you're here or not, and if I snitched, I'd just have double the work. Go. Take however many you want," Ovidio said.

With a smile, Santiago bounded toward the cactus, unsheathing his knife as he went. Looking back to the truck and seeing Ovidio's vigilant eyes, the stout man smiled and danced on the grainy earth. His worn boots kicked up tiny clouds around his feet until he stopped to theatrically smell one of the blood red flowers on the 'holy' thing. Still with his grin, he cut a few prickly pears, ran a lighter over them to singe the thorns, and dropped them into the sweaty bandana he carried. Before Santiago left, he cut a slice of cactus fruit and popped it into his mouth. "Hey," he said still chewing, "you want one? They'll turn you into a real Mexican."

"I'm already a real Mexican," Ovidio replied.

"I've never met a Mexican from El Paso," Santiago laughed. He slammed the rusty door, and they drove back to the large canopy of metal that Pruneda sat under. The trash and scraps they'd left him to clean rotted in the heat around him. When they pulled up, Pruneda was singing.

They did nothing that night around the fire, only watched the stars sit in the sky and listen to the sounds of the land accentuated with the tittering chirps of bats and the distant howl of a coyote mixed with the bellows of a startled cow. Each man had a bottle to himself, and Santiago doused his find with it before eating the pears. He giggled in delight with each chew, reveling in the taste of mischief.

The next morning, Ovidio woke before the rest. He quietly rose from his cot, discarding his coarse blankets and flat pillow, and watched the sun rise. The glowing orb cast long shadows on the ground as if the darkness were being sucked back into the spaces between the stones. Rubbing the bleariness from his eyes, Ovidio burped a fiery reminder of the previous night and stifled it with a large gulp from their jug of water. A groan from behind him had his eyes rolling and his mouth muttering, "Pipe down. I don't smell any worse than you." He turned his eye towards the noise, but no one was awake; Santiago groaned and turned in his creaking cot, which was spotted with fresh sweat. "*Oye*, Santiago!" Ovidio spat, but the man only rolled over and gripped the open shirt he was wrapped in. "Pruneda!" Ovidio shouted, slapping the musician on his ample belly.

"What the hell?" he cried.

"Something's wrong with Santiago," Ovidio told him.

In the morning sun, the heavy rise and fall of his slick chest moved irregularly as they shook him awake with no success. Pruneda wiped his hand on his shirt, then pressed it to the sleeping man's forehead. It dripped when he drew it back.

Ovidio read the man's face easily and checked Santiago's forehead himself; with each second, he shook his head. "Why isn't he burning up?" he asked himself. As he turned to Pruneda, the heaving man shot up in bed, bellowing a scream that sent Ovidio to the floor. The sound was sharp and husky as if born out of hot stone that lay dormant inside his chest. His eyes, half-open, shone a ghastly white with veins painted an unnatural green. They watched Santiago scream into the room with his back tensing to the point of folding over, and his fingers-turned-claws digging rivulets into his ribs.

"What do we do, Ovidio?"

The tall man considered it for a moment, then sighed. "Open all the windows and put the spare blanket on him. You and me will sleep outside until Brizuela comes back."

Santiago got no better, and the screaming fits of mania extended into the nights the two men shared a fire under. Those nights, the land was silent. They tied Santiago to his cot by the wrists and ankles the day before Brizuela returned, but his spasms did not lessen, and all their work did to him was rub his skin raw, staining the ropes red.

"What bit him?" the old man asked, but neither man responded, just watched their friend shiver in bondage. Brizuela looked behind him and snorted. "Worthless," he muttered, then said clearly, "I leave for a week and one of you is half-dead. Worthless." The old man reached down to touch the man's dripping face, but once their skins met, Santiago hissed as if lanced by fire and struggled against his bonds.

He turned his green bordered eyes towards the rancher, seething the words, "*Asesino! Asesino!*" over and over until the hand withdrew.

"Pruneda," Brizuela mumbled, "send for a doctor. Ovidio, let's take a ride."

"What happened to him?" Brizuela asked once they were well enough away from the small brick room turned infirmary.

"I don't know," Ovidio said with his eyes trained ahead.

"Don't bullshit me."

Ovidio gave him a sideward glance, then ran his fingers through his hair. "A few days ago, he went out to find something to eat and came back with some prickly pears. Maybe something bit him while he was out. Knowing Santiago, he wouldn't have said anything anyway."

"Did you check him?" Brizuela asked flatly.

"What?"

"Did you check him for bites? For ticks? For anything?"

"Yes," Ovidio lied.

"Well?"

"We couldn't find anything on him."

"Did you check everywhere?"

"No."

"Why not?"

"We didn't want to strip him down when he was asleep."

"Idiot," Brizuela spat. "Don't want to strip your friend, but you'll let him die on my land easy enough. If I'd been out another day, the three of you would have ruined me. And if he's sick, they'll want to quarantine this whole ranch. More work than help, the bunch of you." They drove the ranch in silence, both thinking of their next move, their next statement, and neither had settled on anything as the truck rolled to a stop before the *caliche* pit. "Stay put," Brizuela said, easing himself out of the truck.

His boots crunched the hard ground as he went, and Ovidio rubbed his moist palms on his jeans. The old man put his face close to the red flowers and, bent and squinting, Brizuela shuffled around the plant as if dancing with an unwilling partner. The ranch hand was glad the old man's eyes were failing him, but, then, the old man stopped and his wrinkled face disappeared behind the thorny discs. His face emerged as a twisted mask with flaring nostrils and a scowl that seemed to reach his lower jaw. Those narrow eyes struck the man like a serpent.

"Fucking Santiago!" Brizuela cursed once in the truck. His leathery hand stroked his chin, and when they pulled up to the sheet metal warehouse, he asked a single question: "Did you know where he got the pears?"

"No."

"Good," Brizuela hissed. "If you had, they'd never find you on this ranch."

It was many hours before Pruneda returned with a doctor, and Brizuela met them well before the physician could enter the rancher's quarters. "Dr. Elizondo," he smiled, "what can we do for you?"

The doctor was old and hunched, leaning to the side he carried his leather medical bag. He adjusted his round lenses that reflected the sun as if his own eyes were burning stars. "Your man here came and told me you've got a sick worker."

Smiling, Brizuela looked at Pruneda and said, "There you go again, getting drunk and making trouble. No, no. No one is sick here." A loud cry came from inside the house and Brizuela laughed as he wrapped his arm around the old doctor and walked him to his truck. "Santiago, he... eh, drank too much and ate too much. A little indigestion put him out for the day. Ah, but you know these migrants, all back and no brain. I wondered if we should call a doctor, but Pruneda was gone before we could call him back." He dipped his head closer to the doctor's ear. "He's really quite simple, but he can play the guitar as good as I've ever heard. Come, I'll tell you all about it on the drive back to town."

Brizuela cast a warning gaze at the two men as he opened the passenger door for Elizondo and held it as he rounded the truck to get in. The old pick-up's rattling rang in their ears before it melted away into the shrieks clawing their way out of Santiago's maddened throat.

"We can't just do nothing," Ovidio said once Brizuela returned.

"I don't want anyone from town coming here. If you want to do something for him, call a priest," Brizuela spat before slamming the door of his ranch house.

The priest and pair of nuns that Pruneda brought from a town thirty miles away asked many questions about the dying man. Under the careful watch of Brizuela, the workers pleaded ignorance, stating that it was something Santiago ate. The old priest, straight and thin in his starched garb, examined Santiago, muttering prayers as he forced the man's eyes open, revealing the thin green membrane that covered his eyes like cataracts born of seeds and nursed with blood. "Where did he get his food?" the priest asked after crossing himself.

"We told you, we didn't know," Brizuela replied.

"I'm aware of your lies. But, if you want to save this man, I need to know everything," the priest said. He crossed his arms over his chest and waited, noting the subtle shivers that rippled through the rancher's weathered face. "Sir, for the love of God, you need to tell me what he ate or else I can do nothing. It is your choice, either let me help him now, or call on me when he needs his last rites."

"I'll show you," Brizuela grumbled after a moment, and they all piled into the pair of trucks together.

"You'll need to bring him," one of the nuns meekly said and an enraged Brizuela roared at his workers to take Santiago along.

Ovidio took the top of the cot, digging his fingers around the pipe-frame, and Pruneda took the bottom. As they lifted him, Santiago convulsed wildly, foaming at the mouth, and barked at them. His moss covered eyes pierced into them, forcing them to turn their faces from him until he was safely in the bed of the truck. They followed Brizuela like a slow moving train, winding its way to the *caliche* pit reluctantly and even with the dirt clouding their windshield and the incessant howling behind them, they noticed the tense strain in Brizuela's shoulders.

They parked the pick-ups next to one another and filed out wordlessly. The two ranch hands eased Santiago out of the truck as the priest carefully made his way towards the cactus and asked Brizuela if it was the offending tree; the old man gave a fierce nod. The priest motioned for the nuns to bring his bag, and once he had it, he placed it on the dusty ground and flipped open the clasps. First, he brought out an old cloth, spreading it out before him like a street vendor and dug further into the plain satchel. On it, he placed a stack of seven thin glass cases, a small flask of holy water, and a small prayer book with a faded crucifix on its leather cover.

Without a word, the nuns took the cases and handed them to Ovidio, telling him to place them in a circle around the pit. "What are these?" he asked as he brought them to the light; they were the pale yellow rose petals.

"When our bishop was on his deathbed, these petals were placed on his skin. The images are gifts from God," the nun said, pointing to the grease spots on them that vaguely formed crude depictions of the Last Supper, the Crucifixion, and the heads of saints. Her round face smiled at him, then she pulled her black rosary from her habit and wrapping it around her wrists, she clapped her hands in prayer and went to stand with her fellows. Ovidio enclosed them in the *caliche* pit with the holy petals, and Pruneda dragged the constraining cot into the ring before he quickly retreated out of it.

The two nuns walked around the rim of the pit, eyes closed and fingers working to ease the black beads out of their hands, with mumbled prayers on their lips. Soon, their chants rose to an audible pitch and Santiago's writhing stopped, but as they ceased and his face relaxed, he shot up again, held by his bonds, and roared at the sky with one clouded eye trained on the priest and his holy water. The priest read from his book, presenting the murky water to the heavens.

With short waves of his arm, he sent the tiny drops of holy water towards the cactus and the flailing prisoner before it. The holy water sizzled on Santiago's chest, drawing an animalistic bellow from his lungs, and the two sisters continued their circuit, though now their eyes never left the flailing man. The priest flung more water followed by blessings and once it touched the brown skin, each drop roiled as if a fire lay slumbering inside the Santiago. From the spray, the plant turned a dying yellow, but soon the tree turned a healthy green as if daring the three members of the clergy. The priest advanced, tossing more water with each step, but all he managed to do was force Santiago to flip over his cot. He stood over the manic man, charged with the good words of his good book, and for a moment, his gaze went to the red flowers.

Inside their delicate petals, he saw writhing faces drawn in organic lines, but mentally pushed them aside as a trick of the eyes until one infantile face spread its lips in a smile. Each of the blood red petals seemed alive, forming curses with their painted mouths, and some of them bared their soft teeth to hiss at the holy man. As if connected by something ethereal, Santiago took up the same grin with a harsh laugh that seemed to never end. He turned his veined eyes on Brizuela and opened his mindless mouth wider, puffing a cloud of the white dust with each huff that rattled his bindings.

The sisters quickened their pace around him with furrowed brows and eyes shut. Their hands shook as the laughter continued. Both women looked at their rosaries in horror before the holy glass cases shattered and the rosary beads burst in all directions. A single black bead rolled at Ovidio's feet. As he retrieved it, his hand hung in the air. The bead shook and sprouted tiny legs that clawed at the sky as its round belly formed a bloated red hourglass. The beads turned themselves over on their spider legs and scuttled towards the priest, moving around Santiago's giggling shoulders as if he were only a stone. He threw holy water at them in the form of a cross, but still they chased him until he and his flock were out of the pit, huffing and wheezing. "Where did this come from?" the priest blathered. "Where in God's name did you get this foul thing?"

"It grew there," Brizuela spoke, his scowl chiseled on his face.

The priest turned a frightened eye on the cactus and said, "I can do nothing for you. I'll have no more to do with you or your lands."

"So, my man is to die?"

The priest stuttered, unable to speak a word from the chill his blood took from the plant, but one of the shivering nuns spoke for him. "I know of someone. She is an old *curandera*," she said and the father's face warped with confusion, but he did not stop her. "In New Mexico, the people believe she is powerful. Maybe she," the middle-aged woman said as she crossed herself, "can rid you of this plant."

Brizuela ran his fingers in and out of his moustache for a moment. "Call her then. Maybe she'll make it before Santiago laughs himself to death."

Two days later, the scene was the same except the priest had turned into an old woman with a face marred by time's unforgiving hand and a waist inflated to be at an even level with her plump breasts. Beside her, a small boy, no older than seven, held on to a small pouch of herbs until his knuckles turned white, and Santiago lay at the feet of the flowering cactus like a reluctant sacrifice, now half-starved and wild. When he yelled to the sky and snapped his bonds taut, the boy reflexively grabbed the old witch's dress and hid behind it.

She watched the man wriggle on the cot for a moment before she moved towards him, slipping the bag of herbs out of the boy's hands. "Don't worry, little Antonio, it will be all right. The land can cure a man infected by it," she said, tussling his hair with a smile. Once inside the ring, the witch opened the pouch, took pinches of herbs in her hand, and mixed the dried stuff in her palm. She moved towards Santiago who leered at her with a crooked smile and predatory eyes. "You don't scare me," she announced, thrusting her hand on his chest, which heaved at the touch of her stubby, calloused fingers. Yet, for all his shaking and the murderous look he gave her, a wave of serenity washed over him. She prayed to herself as the boy watched silently and when Santiago's eyes rolled back in his head, she thrust her fingers into his mouth, placing the herbs on his tongue.

He sucked at her fingers like a newborn calf.

"Ah," she smiled, "you see little Antonio, nothing to be afraid—"

Santiago's teeth clamped down on her fingers and his lips curled back, letting the herb speckled froth dribble out of the corners of his mouth. The old witch screamed and beat her round fist about his head as the wind kicked up dust and roared in their ears. Pruneda and Ovidio, backed by a yelling Brizuela, tore into the ring and opened Santiago's jaw like an old bear trap. It took Pruneda pulling on the top of Santiago's face and Ovidio at the bottom to pry it open enough for the *curandera* to slip her bloody fingers out and once Santiago's mouth was empty, the laughing began again. Each belly jiggling spurt sent specks of ruby red blood into the air, which grew dark and thick as if the very space around them were injected with a foul ink.

Though the evening was far off, the *caliche* pit was overrun with darkness born of the grey clouds swelling above their heads like a virus spreading over the acres of the ranch. Inside the puffy walls, lightning glowed, and the booming bursts that followed deafened them to all but the laughter. The trucks shook from the wind whipping through their clothes and the little boy was thankful no one noticed the wet stain growing on his pants. The rusted tools shook and scraped inside the truck beds. Amidst the maelstrom, the old witch raised her hand for her prayers, but a streak of red lightning struck the flowering cactus squarely.

The blinding force sent them all to the ground to backtrack like spiders and though they all shook in fear, they could not stop watching the display before them. The clouds sent bolt after bolt of chain lightning down around the pit, filling their vision with white energy, and the boy's stain grew volumes once the black shadow of a woman formed and danced on the cactus plates as if they were wooden planks. The ghastly hair whipped about her head as her black feet touched the thorns and sprung up again with her thin arms up to the raging sky. For the first time, in the sight of the feminine shadow, Brizuela was truly silent.

The sky rained lightning and she danced.

The old man whispered something none of them understood, and the shadow stopped her turning and leveled both her colorless eyes at the rancher. Brizuela retreated from her pointing finger, which did not move once it found him, and stammered neither English nor Spanish. The shadow's eyes seemed to narrow and it threw its head back, letting loose a scream. The bolts branched out, striking the land in unforgiving barrages, yet there was no smoke, no fires, simply the deafening fury of the air. Ovidio called out for the old woman to get to one of the trucks, but found she was already under one, smothering her grandson under her loose girth. Still, Ovidio yelled at them though his words were decimated by the vicious air. He felt a hand on his shoulder and fought against its pull. "Move it! Run!" Brizuela yelled in his ear.

"But, Santiago—"

"Leave him! We can do nothing!" the old man countered.

With one final look, Ovidio scrambled with the rest of them to the trucks, and it took all three of them to pull the old witch from under her transportable awning. The trucks sped down the roads with lightning lighting the sky behind them, and their blood seemed to stop when Ovidio noticed the murky woman pointing at their backs with Santiago laughing at her feet.

Brizuela stopped the truck in front of the worker's house and told them all to get out, but no one moved. "I thought I told you to move!"

"We can't stay in there," Pruneda said frantically as the sky, still inky black, loosed bolts of electricity.

"And why the hell not?" Brizuela spat.

"Sir," Ovidio interrupted as he came up to the window. "Our house has a metal roof on it." All three men looked up at the sheet metal roof, and the man growled to himself as he rubbed his grizzled chin. "Do you really want to put out a *curandera*, sir?" Again, all eyes moved together, focusing on the old woman whose grandson wept between her pendulous breasts in tiny squeals.

"Fine, but I swear if you touch anything, *anything*, I'll wrap you in foil and send you out there to fetch Santiago, understand?" he grumbled, and they all nodded. Brizuela drove a little further, and the five of them ran into his small ranch house. Once inside, they broke into pairs: the witch and her screaming child, Pruneda and Ovidio, and Brizuela with his foul mood, which he took with him into his bedroom. No one in the large living room-kitchen combo moved until they heard the snap of a lock.

"What do you think it is, Ovidio?"

The tall man pulled up a chair, but said nothing. The child cried loudly as the old woman tried to comfort him. "Shhh. *Ya mijo, ya. No hay bultos aqui. Ya chiquito, no llores. Ya, ya, no pasa nada. Todo está bien.*" The two workers watched her as she stroked his hair with a shaking hand, and they knew from the look in her old face that she had no problem lying to her own flesh and blood.

"Do you think it's true? Do you think there is a ghost?" Pruneda pressed barely above a whisper.

"I don't know. I've never seen anything like it. But, why ask me?"

"You're the smart one."

"Why?"

"Well, you read."

"Ah," Ovidio scoffed as he rose, "I read comic books, Pruneda. I've never read a book without pictures." He moved past his friend as the lights danced outside of the small, square windows. The brief intensity of the lights showed pictures of Angus and land on the walls in no order. There were no children nor anyone who looked like the old man inside of the frames, but there was one picture that nearly sent Ovidio to the tile floor laughing: Brizuela's wedding portrait. Though the photographed man had the same moustache across his face, he stood straighter and in a frilly blue tuxedo. He held hands with a woman too young and too beautiful for him. Her hair was down to the middle of her back and her large eyes shone bright from the reports of falling light. A feathered dream-catcher dangled from one of her ears. There was something about her shape, her stance, that struck him as chillingly familiar, though he'd never seen his boss with the shining wedding band on his finger.

"*Chinga!*" Brizuela fumed as he unlocked the door. "Will that kid ever shut up!" He strode up to the sitting family with his balled fists on his belt. "Thank God or whatever you believe in that I don't have to put up with this for long. What's he so afraid of? It's not like he lives here. I live here! I have that, that thing, on my land!"

"Boss," Pruneda said coming up behind him, "leave them alone. He's only a boy."

"Ah, a boy who's getting piss on my floor."

"*Señor*—" the old woman started.

"Don't talk to me. Do you know how much it cost me to get you here? No. You're damn children should've just stolen my wallet and for you to do what? Crowd my home. You want my sympathy? I don't have any to give. I don't know how they do it in New Mexico, but this is Texas; this is a hard land. The strong live here and the weak," he said eyeing the small boy, "have no business drowning my land in tears."

"You are a monster," the old woman finally said, gripping her child tighter. "Have you no heart?"

"I buried my heart in this land years ago," Brizuela scoffed before returning to the darkness of his room, leaving them to the natural strobe light of an angry sky and their thoughts.

Pruneda left the next morning to drop off the old woman and her child in town with enough money to send them on a bus back home. Brizuela, still white knuckled and tight faced, took Ovidio to the *caliche* pit and expected to see a corpse bound to a cot. Yet the first thing they saw was a white owl perched on the lone cactus, watching over the sleeping man. The torn carcasses of snakes and field mice were scattered all around. When they neared it, the albino bird did not move and they dared not touch it. They collected Santiago and left under its vigilant eyes.

That day there were no wisps of smoke in the distance, only flying rings of vultures over a single pasture, and it was the birds breaking from the groups to meander to the ground that led the three men to investigate. At first, Brizuela saw nothing in the thin brush line, but the birds flying overhead were too much to ignore, and he yelled out of the window for Pruneda and Ovidio to keep their eyes open. The stink of something burnt and foul filled both the air and the cab as the group turned along the two grooves of a road; the truck stopped as a dozen vultures burst into the air, hissing at their meal's interruption.

At the sight before the truck, Brizuela slammed his fist on the steering wheel and screamed, "I'm ruined! That damn *bruja* ruined me!"

Neither of the ranch-hands knew what to make of it. They'd seen hundreds if not thousands of bulls in all shapes and breeds, but had never know a bull to die the way Brizuela's had. The black angus skin was charred to match the fur that now blew away in scorched clumps, sticking to mesquite trees and buffel grass alike, while its four legs stuck straight up in the air like an overturned table. Its face was warped in an agonized howl stopped in time and its ocular fluid spilled out of its open eyelids to be soaked up by the soil. Tiny holes, releasing the rotten gases of its cooked innards, peppered its bloated stomach.

"What am I paying you idiots for? Get down and look at it!" Brizuela complained and they obeyed.

"What do you expect us to do?" Ovidio asked as he crossed the old man's window.

"See if you can move it."

"It weighs over a thousand pounds," Ovidio countered.

"Then try really hard," Brizuela growled.

The two men wiped their sweating faces and rubbed the perspiration on their hands as they stared down at the bull. Each man took a side, Pruneda pushing the hind legs and Ovidio pulling the fore legs. Once they forced the stiff limbs into movement, the bones cracked like dry branches, sending Pruneda barreling down onto the pregnant belly and Ovidio falling backwards into a thorny bush. They only slightly heard Brizuela's curses over their own. Pruneda placed his large hand onto the inflated stomach to push himself up, but with the weight concentrated onto his palm, the crispy skin gave way, sending his arm further into the visceral soup and a noxious wave of air up to his nose. The musician shuddered as he slipped in the slick mess and vomited onto the burnt underbelly of the beast and brought both hands to his face to catch his regurgitation, but did nothing more than scatter the flood into a shower. Ovidio moved to his feet, but Brizuela pushed him to the ground as he passed.

"What's the matter with you?" he shouted at Pruneda, who trembled and the long threads of mucus vibrated like harp strings with each dry heave.

Ovidio stood, plucking the thorns out of his elbows, when the old man let his boot fly at the shivering man who couldn't find the strength to push himself out of the sun baked stink. He started to tell Brizuela to calm down, but the old man spun on his heel and beat him to the first word. "You shut your fucking mouth! You want to stick up for him? Eh? I'm paying you two and you do nothing but bring me misery," he accentuated the word with another swift kick behind him. "I've got a dying man on my land and the expenses of a priest and a worthless witch! For what! To have this *payaso* get sick at the sight of one of my, *my*," he repeated tapping his chest with his wrinkled forefinger, "dead bulls. And if he can't take the work he creates for himself, then he can get his worthless ass away from here. You hear that Pruneda! Pack that stupid banjo and go back to Monterrey!"

The old man took one look at Pruneda's shocked face and scoffed at the sight of the prostrated man. "And if neither of you can move this thing, then I'll do it my damned self." He pushed past Ovidio and moved towards the truck, grumbling to himself.

Pruneda stayed on his knees as if frozen, and Ovidio followed the old man determined. "Brizuela! You can't fire Pruneda. He's done nothing but do what you've told him to." The old man did not acknowledge him, only looked through the bed of his truck. "He's got a family you heartless bastard!" he said and hesitated though Brizuela made no move that he heard him. "I swear to God, if you fire that man, I'll report you! They'll take everything from you! I'll—" he stuttered when the old man turned, and his arm went for his rifle inside the truck.

Ovidio backed up a step with his hands waving between them and tried to explain himself in nervous laughs, but the old man advanced with his eyes past the tall man and with a tooth revealing sneer, he cocked his rifle.

"What the hell is it now?" Brizuela asked himself, and Ovidio followed his eyes to the white owl flying out into the brush away from the *caliche* pit. "In the truck! In the truck! The both of you!" he hissed and hobbled quickly into it, hardly waiting for Pruneda to get both legs in the bed before planting his foot on the gas. The truck tumbled through the uneven roads and the two hired hands ducked from the low hanging branches striking the roof of the truck and showering them in stripped leaves and splintered thorns. Each turn sent one into the other and the tools mingled with their turning bodies, scraping their elbows and forearms with rusted claws and dingy fangs. When it felt as though they could only tempt fate for a moment longer before a pick-axe bore a hole in their heads or a pitchfork prong found their cheeks, the truck ground to a halt. The two ranch hands were untangled fast enough to see a group of ragged men with black matted hair and bare feet caked with dirt up to their ankles run from the *caliche* pit into the wilderness, braving the needles of foliage tearing at their leathery skin.

Yet, even with Brizuela spitting fire as he got off the truck, one man did not run. "*Disculpe, señor,*" he said over his shoulder with a smile, "*yo nada más quiero una tuna.*" He reached out and plucked a bulb off the cactus easily, shaved a spot clean with a rusty skinning knife, and sank his square teeth into it. His dried lips parted further in a smile with each slow chew which set Brizuela's teeth, forcing him to level his Winchester. Though the click of the hammer struck the ranch-hand's ears same as a funeral bell, the lone man paid no attention to it.

"*Lárgate!*" the old man shouted from behind his shaky rifle, but the heedless man bit into the fruit again. Brizuela tried to keep the man in his sights, but his age rumbled through the stock, and he squinted to no avail. He pushed the rifle into Pruneda's arms. "Shoot him! If you want your job, shoot him!" he yelled into the musician's ear, but the frightened man could barely keep the gun off the floor, let alone fire it.

"Brizuela," Ovidio started as he placed his hand on Pruneda's shoulder. The old man shot him a look and shoved the rifle into his hands, reciting the same warning to him. "But sir—"

"Bah!" Brizuela said with an eye on the eating traveler. "A man of words is just that: words! Nothing but excuses for not doing what needs to be done!" he spat and snatched the rifle back. Despite his wobbling arm and the protests of his men, the old man fired once, missing the traveler by inches and the bullet bounced flawlessly off the cactus to be lost in its thorny mass. With mouth full, the man spun around begging, but Brizuela chambered another round which fired straight into the man's lung, blasting a gushing hole into his ribs; the force sent him in a tangled heap onto the unmoving tree. The old man lowered his weapon, advancing to the gurgling man splayed across the blooming cactus. He watched the sightless eyes search for God in the sky before the body was finally still.

As his wrinkled hand drew closer, the dead man's mouth opened wide, sucking in the air like a vacuum that never ceased, never filled. He inhaled all that could be funneled into his lungs until his very arms tried to pry themselves away from their impaled trappings. Out of the hole, the men heard a sharp whistle grow. The sound intensified into a bleating and as the old man retreated a step, a green bulb inflated out of the wound. The cactus bulb drank the spilling blood and fattened, growing thorns that stabbed mercilessly into the dead flesh, and finally blossomed in a delicate red flower as if the fallen man were no more than fertile ground. Once the unholy flower struck the apex of its growth, each petal flew off its root to spin insect-like in the air inside the *caliche* pit. The red petals flew in symmetry, drawing lines in the air with their speed and spun around with a wind that only filled the grainy borders of the pit.

None of the men noticed the weight of invisible feet sinking in the ground until a single petal struck the invisible form in its flight. It flattened against the unseen obstacle and with the one, more followed, plastering to translucent flesh like a child's puzzle. They framed slender shoulders and a small waist before the soft petals slapped against a lithe cheeks and a small, graceful forehead. The body upon the tree withered until the cyclone was complete, and a woman made of flowers stood before the thin carcass of a mummified man.

Ovidio looked at the figure taking light steps towards the rancher and noted her shape, swearing to himself that he knew it. And from the shaking of the old man's lip, the tear in his eye, he knew it too. "*Cómo?*" Brizuela sputtered and the specter opened its hollow eyes.

"*Esta es la fruta que usted plantó,*" it spoke with a voice of dried leaves scratching in the wind. It stared at the old man for a moment and its leafy lips spread. "*Usted lo recuerda. Usted no lo puede olvidar.*" Cocking its head to one side on its slender neck, it reached out to him, caressing his cheek. "*Tu quieres que ningun hombre me encuentre, pero muchos lo han echo. Tu quieres que nada más te mire a ti, que nada más seamos nosotros dos. Cómo tu desees,*" it spoke as its hands brought Brizuela's face closer to its own. The old man smelt the sweet fragrance off its puckered lips. His old face swelled from the scent, and neither man had known the rancher was capable of an expression of joy nor the twisted mask of fright it shifted into as his weathered eyes swallowed the sight of the specter's mouth unhinging, expanding like a viper's, and the spinning, ever spinning, jumble of yellow thorns, rowed like teeth into the blackness of its maw.

It took hold of the old man's hand by the wrist and used its other hand to push his gray head aside before it bit down on his collar. Each of the spinning thorns sent another gurgling scream out of the rancher as he convulsed awkwardly in its vice-like grip. Blood dripped in heavy drops from her flowered lips as the apparition reveled in the hot taste of it through the unseen roots of its body. As it descended again, it noted the two ranch-hands who could only move away from the pit one cautious step at a time. Its lips curled back. The moving thorns spun at them through its wide smile. "*Quieres mi fruta,*" it laughed coyly only to clamp down harder on the old man.

Ovidio pushed Pruneda into the truck and put it in gear. He dared not pass its eyes, but as he sent the truck into a backwards sprint, he thought they found his own. In his wild backtracking, they knocked over a T-post, sending strings of old barbed wire down onto Cazares soil, yet they did not think to fix it, only to turn the truck around and fly straight to the county road.

"*Chinga*," Pruneda muttered; Ovidio only nodded for him to continue. "Who is going to pay us for this?"

"You're a damn fool, Pruneda, if you think we came out with the worst of it," Ovidio replied and pointed down the road. Climbing down the hill, Santiago laughed at the sky as he dragged his cot by his bloody wrist.

—ETC.—

The Grinding Business

I know what you're thinking. It's all right. Get it all the time. But, it ain't a bad business. Bones.

Yes, there's an unholy stink about the place, but bone grinding's done me a lot of good over the years. It's in more things than people would ordinarily imagine. Bones. Gelatin, for instance. That's what gets most people. I can't say how many times I've gone up to someone—a momma and kid or some old man in a hospital—and tell them that spoon of wiggling color is ground up bones and couple of drops of food coloring. I could talk all night about the faces they give me when I tell them that. And I would if my beer wasn't running out.

Well, more often than not, there's bones in sugar, too. I've been supplying local places with bone powder to make their sugar white for years. The market on bone ash west of the Colorado, I had that cornered. Lots of old ladies want to learn to paint china so they can guilt their kids into keeping them long after they've gone. Can't tell you how many bone-china plates get carved up on account of kids eating canned spaghetti and chicken fingers off them. No respect, I say.

But, it's been good to me. The grinding business. Along with what regular folk need, there's the farmers. Whenever the winds start blowing from the north, the heat cuts down about ten degrees, then they're running here. The farmers. Some of the old ones, they still bring in horse-carts. They want that bone-meal, you see. Can't get enough of it during planting season. But, I always warn them. Don't go sprinkling that stuff around like it was salt on eggs. Every varmint and coyote for twenty miles will catch that stench in the wind. Once, Jim Farleigh, he bought two fifty pound sacks of bone-meal—I know it sounds like a lot of bone, but any cow that's lived a year can yield more bone than that, if it's processed right. Well,

Jim mixed it with soil and threw the mix out on the fields. Gave them a spruce watering.

Jim ain't with us anymore, so I won't go making any judgments about it. But, I warned him. I always warn them.

Jim woke up the next morning, not with his old rooster, Remus, neither. Woke up with the sun. Jim used to have a habit of taking a pinch of chew the minute he woke up. If he lived, I suspect all his teeth would be rot by now. Anyway, he took his pinch of chew, put it up against his cheek, and made a cup of coffee. I don't know what he heard, but some sound got him to go outside. When he opened that door, there were wolves uprooting his crops. I don't really know why Jim tried to spook them with a broom. Guess it was all that was handy. I'd've fetched a shotgun or a shovel, at least. All they found was blood at first, but a tracker, one set on the old ways, he followed a buzzard and found enough of Jim to be identified.

Hardly enough to be buried, though.

I always say to mix the bones with the dirt and let them sit for a week. Keeps the smell down and give the bones time to soften up a bit. Bleeds the nutrients better. Plus, all San Casimiro county won't smell like my place for a month, causing all types of hell with animals. And that's what I was doing there in the middle of the night, watching for possums or coyotes or something. Earl, the line manager, told me he's been finding the Bone Room out of order in the mornings. Been that way for two weeks, so he said. Don't really know how he can tell, to be quite honest.

The Bone Room is what it sounds like. Just one big square room piled up to the ceiling with bones. It's got a chute leading in from the outside for the deliveries. The tiles aren't blue anymore, more of a dingy green now. We'd take all the bones from every butcher for thirty miles. People are often surprised by how many butchers there are around here, when the weather's good at least. We throw all manner of bones in that room. Skulls and legs and ribs and spines. Hell, I never did learn all the bones. Too damn many and it's not like all animals have the same kind. The only bones I never kept were teeth. Boar tusks and pig teeth and thick old cow molars. I've got the South Texas market on teeth. I really don't know what those *curanderas* do with them, but they pay me and bless me—so they say—and that's enough for me. Anything for the customer.

Reminds me of the one tooth I carry round my neck. My pappy gave it to me on the happiest day of his business career. It was the day Mr. Harold Hemming, the owner of Hemming's Grinder and Bone Inc., left town. Strange, he never closed up the shop, put it up for sale. Nothing like that. Just went and disappeared one day, no clue to where he'd run off to. My old man, he went and took an old pig's tooth—a small one if you ask me—and put a silver loop on it. I've had to change the chain a few times over the years, but I still carry it to this day. And though I found it weird that Mr. Hemming just took off on his wife and business, it didn't bother me because I didn't like Mr. Hemming much. He used to tussle my hair like I was a kid even when I was thirteen and say, "Well, howdy little Rich?" on account of me being named Richard, after my father. Always had a habit of clicking his teeth after he said it. I hated that clack, clack, clack. To this day it bothers me to think about it...

About thirty years to the month since I saw that old man.

But, I'm moving all types of ways except forward. When Earl told me about the Bone Room, I just said to put some mousetraps around or a couple of wire-nooses for the raccoons. That's why I had that shotgun. Earl told me it sure as hell wasn't no raccoon, though. No raccoon he'd ever seen could toss a cow skull hard enough to break it against the wall. Wasn't mice neither. Mice, they don't go for the bones we can see. No, they want the choice chunks of meat and any marrow left over. The butchers they use now, no ethics. They just hack away at the cattle and pigs, couldn't care less if they're leaving two pounds of meat on each leg or if they break the floating rib out of carelessness. Those mice though, they sure like that people these days are lazy as all hell. They'll scuttle in those bones, down to the deepest, smelliest part and set up roost there. Plenty to eat. Rotten meat and all manner of bugs that crawl in there.

That smell, it'll bring every flesh eater for twenty miles. I guarantee it.

Some of the other workers, well, it's either Inish or Inez, really. Other than one man to run the steam baths and another to separate the bones from the gunk, there's not much demand for help in the grinding business. Inish, he moves the bones from the Bone Room to the lines, where Inez bathes them in a steam bath once, cleans the excess flesh and hair and whatever other type of nastiness, and bathes them again. From there, slap the bones on a conveyer belt and they'll get tossed into the heater to dry. Then, off to the grinder.

I remember it took me what seemed like a decade to get used to that stink. Think, wet bones and dry bones from a hundred animals getting wedged between two millstones and ground up. I heard a man compare it to someone having collected toenails and tossed them in a fire, but I had to wonder how he'd even know what a burning toenail smelled like. To this day though, I can't think of any better way to put it.

Hell, it's still bothering me now. It's a stink that settles in the back of your throat and won't budge. That's how we lost the last line-manager. He'd go down to Rosita's and drink and drink. Nearly clear the place of whiskey every night just trying to chase that stink out of his throat. He'd show up so hung-over that once his overalls caught on the conveyer. He was too drunk to scream, but thank the lord he was too fat to fit through the opening. I came in to find him holding on for dear life, gleaming white bones piling up on him as they were coming from Inez's station. I suppose, if he hadn't of nearly killed himself, it would have been one hell of a sight. I chuckle now and again, picturing him on the belt, slurring as all manners of bones covered him like so much sand or something.

But, Inez and Inish, too, they've been telling me they hear things in that place. Weird things. Like bones rattling together. I had a good laugh when they told me. 'It's a bone grinding facility,' I said. 'I'd expect that some bones might rattle from time to time. And with the varmints we get in here during the summers, it's nothing to worry about.' A mouse or two can knock over an ill-stacked set of bones and make one hell of a row. Earl though, he said that cow skull was proof it wasn't some little mouse. Nor something bigger. Even if someone found a cow skull out in the *monte* and took the biggest rock they could find, they'd break it all right, but not shatter the thing. Earl, he hunted down most of the pieces of that skull and tried to put them together. Someone would've needed a jackhammer to do that to a cow skull.

In the night, I heard something. Something like the clatter of bones falling on concrete. It came from the Bone Room. An empty rattle like all the bones were getting rolled around. Sounded like whatever was in there had something specific on its mind.

I didn't need to pull the hammers on my shotgun. I'm not a superstitious man, but staying in a place with a room full of bones overnight never sat too well with me. Going out into the hall from my office, the sound got louder. The walls were funneling it out to me at such a volume, I shouldered that shotgun like I'd need to blast my way through that empty place. Something—ribs by the crack of them—hit the Bone Room door from the inside. I almost pulled the trigger right there. Usually, I wouldn't admit such a thing, but I don't see the harm in it now, thinking back on it.

Just a basic human reaction.

I went to the door slow, listening to whatever was in there tear through the place. Made sure it wasn't just on the other side. I'll tell you, before I heard it and a hell of a long time before I saw it, I meant to open the door quick and shoot down or up or wherever the critter was. That was until I heard a fast crack of bone on bone and got the tingle from hearing at least fifteen bones snap. Don't care if a man has owned a grinding business for a hundred years, no one gets used to that sound. Fifteen bones at least...

I opened that door quick. That part, I got right. But, I didn't even aim, just used the door like a shield and fired. Damn near tore the gun out of my hand. Couldn't hear much after that. Nowhere for the boom to go but my damn ears. Left them ringing ever since. Even talking now, if a word don't sound right, blame the ringing not the drinking.

The flies that came tearing out of that place, it felt like the Lord's anger on the Egyptians. Thousands of them buzzing, their wings burning on account of the buckshot. Even with the ringing in my ears, the flies were always there. I didn't need to hear it. Enough flies come around, they move so much air, a man can feel it. Like the world's electric.

Anyway, I'd shot.

The sound had stopped, from what I could tell, but, as I said, my hearing was and is questionable.

Looking in, I expected a bear from the sounds or a cougar, maybe. But, there wasn't anything but a smelly old room filled up to the ceiling with bones. I watched for a long time, hoping to see something that could explain it. Some animal crawling out from the pile or a burglar shitting his pants. But, no such luck. Not a damn thing. Took a step in and poked at some of the bones. Flies were hopping from one stinking set of bones to the other.

Thud.

I wheeled around and shot again.

Bones trembled and shattered, but I didn't have to do any waiting for something to move. It was a thick cow spine with the shoulders of a horse. Wriggling like a snake, it rattled against the other filthy bones and other, other bits of bones came tumbling to it. Rib bones and femurs and hooves started collecting and configuring until that thing, that wriggling spine, was able to sit itself up.

I was pulling the trigger the whole time. Couldn't even remember there were no shells in the gun.

It didn't have a head, but I swear it swung around to face me.

One of the hands, all made up of small bits of busted tibias and broken ribs, dove into the piles and came up with a toothless pig's skull, jaw and all. Still had some fur and gore caked on it. Whatever that thing was, it slapped that on its neck and stared at me with those empty eyes. By god, it reached out for me, jaws working like it was trying to speak, trying to tunnel its awful rattling through its stolen ribs. Then, like a trio of bullets. Clack. Clack. Clack.

The damn thing was snapping at me.

I threw the damn shotgun at it and ran out of there. Never went back. The bone grinding business was good to me, no doubt. My old man taught me everything he knew about it and he knew it all. But, he sure as hell never said something like that was going to happen. I'm a little embarrassed to say it, but I don't see any harm in it now. Not when I think back to that abomination snapping at me like some turtle. Reaching out to me with that shaky claw.

Damn, it's going to take a few more beers to get that thought out of my head...

—ETC.—

A Boy and His Mud Man

While his grandfather was out at Bare Back's Gentlemen's Club, little Marcus Towers III left the ranch house ready for a proper adventure. He was dressed in a set of faded dungarees and a overly starched cotton shirt. Broken in the crook of his arm was his single barrel shot gun; in his back pocket was his late father's notched Bowie knife. It was late April and the snakes were coming out of their holes to warm themselves in the sun, the old Mexican ranch-hand, Jose, told him in scratchy Spanish. Marcus only nodded to the ranch-hand and set out anyway.

The ranch—Ranchos Los Edmundos, though Marcus could never figure out why the ranch was named as such—was not a large one. Twenty or so acres of dry *monte* with a few head of cattle and an old Appaloosa named Don Juan. San Casimiro county was in the middle of its worst drought and out of the two small watering tanks, only one had a puddle of murky water in the center of it. Marcus wanted to go to it in hopes of shooting at a duck returning north for the spring. The air was fragrant with the smell of huisache and cacti and the boy was not out of sight of the ranch house before tiny beads of perspiration bubbled onto his forehead. He wiped at it without a thought, keeping his eyes keen on the ground and bushes.

The path he took was not too overgrown and he stayed on the rut his grandfather's truck made when he did his ranch work, which was seldom. More often than not, the Mexican ranch-hand was the one doing the working and the driving and the feeding and the moving of animals from one pasture to another. As he walked, a few doves and a scissortail flew from the dry grass, calling excitedly in the air. He fixed his shotgun, aimed, but stopped. The birds were too far away to shoot and even if he hit one, little Marcus would not chance walking in the chest-high grass unless he was on Don Juan, but the old horse seldom did more than eat and shit in the corral.

On the way into the *monte*, Marcus passed the one place he was never to go. The dump. It was a dug out surrounded by stout trees filled with spider webs and little seed pods. Through the dried brush, there sat a rusted washing machine and broken strings of barbed wire stuck out along with a broken closet door. A glittering array of broken beer bottles of every color and hue painted the sides of the pit like a dingy lightshow. Marcus's grandfather, Marcus Senior, told him never to play there. Too many things to cut himself with. Too many nests for snakes and deadly spiders.

Marcus kept to the path and passed one of the stock tanks. It was a deep depression in the ground, the dirt cracked from the constant sun and not so constant rain. From the hill where he stood, Marcus could make out a few empty turtle shells and bits of white moss, dried out and dead. In the center of the tank were some bricks laid out like broken teeth. At first, Marcus wanted to make his way down the hill to look at the empty turtle shells, but remembered that once the Mexican ranch-hand had told him rattlers and the like tended to stick by dried ponds to catch frogs and other critters looking for some reprieve from the heat. But, little Marcus stood there and looked at it anyway. Once, so he'd been told, the tanks were full of dark water and all kinds of birds would flock to it and drink among the cattle. Little Marcus wished he could have seen it.

He moved across the hill, keeping the tank in his sight. In the afternoon sun, there was a glint of red in the center of the stock tank. At first, Marcus thought it was a trick of the light. Often at the ranch, a bit of dew on the leaves of a mesquite tree or a bit of sap on a cactus glittered in the sun. But, that was rare. Rain was needed for those tricks of the light. He stopped, his shadow stretching out to the dried lake, elongated and cartoonishly thin. The boy moved his head from side to side, trying to recreate the red light. To his amazement, the glint was constant no matter how much he moved his head. He assembled his shotgun, flipped the safety off, and went down.

He took a dried stick off a tree and used it to tap on the ground. A few flick-bugs and horse-flies danced in the air before overheating in the sun and finding other shady spots. It was so hot, not even the mosquitoes were hanging around the barren watering hole. He got to the rim of the tank, the place where water had met the land, and tapped at the ground with his stick. It seemed firm enough. The boy knew he wouldn't sink in and track caked on mud into the house later. He fitted the stick into a crack in the dirt and advanced like the soldiers he'd seen on the old television set: barrel down, finger close but not touching the trigger. Ever ready.

Skittishly, he advanced a few steps, stopped, and found the red glint in the dirt amidst the bricks. He'd move a few steps, look around for anything that resembled a snake, and continue. It took him five minutes to get to the spot he'd seen from the hill.

When he came to it, it looked like a wet stone eye. Perfectly round and moist. Marcus looked at it for a moment, and crouched down, covering it with his shadow.

"Thank you," Marcus heard the ground say and the eye seemed to blink before focusing on him.

Little Marcus drew back screaming and shot the red stone with a barrel of tiny shot. The ground broke and dust went up in a tiny cloud to be blown away by the small breeze. With shaking hands, the boy went through his pockets and reloaded the shotgun. He aimed it and watched the broken spot.

At first, nothing happened and he wondered if it was simply a trick he played on himself. The old Mexican had told him not to go out without a wide-brimmed hat. The sun had a way of making a person crazy just by being there and in San Casimiro, the sun was always there, even at night.

Marcus had just lowered his shotgun, rubbing his eyes with his dirty fingers.

"Why did you do that, little boy?" a voice said. It was an earthy sound that seemed to come from grains of dust rubbing against one another.

When Marcus looked back to the spot, the chips of the red eye were coming together again until there was a pupil and retina. Beneath it, a mouth formed in the cracks of the dirt and moved little, but it did move.

"I asked you a question, boy," the eye in the dirt said. "Why would you shoot me after I thanked you? It hardly seems like the right thing to do."

"Well," little Marcus said. "You scared me, that's all. I don't come up on talking eyeballs usually."

The eye looked him over and narrowed a bit. "Could you please move back where you were. I've been in the sun for so long," it said.

Marcus moved and stooped to look at the creature. "What are you?"

"My, my," the dirt mouth whispered. "That is not a rude question at all."

"Didn't mean to be," Marcus said.

"Just as you didn't mean to shoot me in the eye, I suppose," the dirt mouth hissed, but it was not an aggressive sound like the possums that sometimes went through the trash. It sounded like laughter. "But, to answer your question, little boy, I don't know what I am."

"How come you don't know? I figured everyone knew what they were," Marcus said.

"Do you know who you are?" the dirt mouth asked and the corners of it slowly formed a smile.

"Heck yes I do," little Marcus said. "I'm Marcus Towers the third, pleased to meet you."

The eye widened and narrowed again. "Hello Marcus," the dirt mouth said up to him. "I'm glad to meet you. But, it does not change the fact that I do not know who or what I am."

"No one ever told you?" Marcus asked.

"I do not have many visitors here," the voice said. "But, I do remember flashes from time to time. I sometimes see a woman and two children. Little girls. They seem…happy. I enjoy seeing them, though it is seldom."

"Well, what else do you see?" Marcus asked.

"The sun and the moon, mostly," the voice said. "I hear many things, though. Feel many things."

"Like what?"

"The land," the voice said. The stone eye seemed to focus out beyond Marcus or beneath the ground, the boy could not tell. "It is not happy. It is poisoned."

"It don't seemed poisoned to me," Marcus said and looked out to the land. "A little dry, maybe."

"It is very dry," the dirt mouth said. The eye seemed to think before it spoke again. "Marcus," it said. "Could you please do something for me? It is not a large task."

"Well, my daddy always told me to hear it first and agree to it second," little Marcus said.

"Your father was a wise man," the dirt mouth rasped. "All I want you to do is bring me some water. It doesn't have to be much. Just something to slake my throat. Please."

"Well," Marcus said and scratched his head. He looked up at the sun and figured his grandfather wouldn't be back for hours. "Yeah," he said. "I can do that for you."

"Thank you," the voice said and the eye seemed to close. As Marcus made his way back to the stick he wedged in the dirt, the voice called out to him. When the boy came back, the eye was looking up at him. "You said your name was Marcus Towers…the third?"

"Yep, that's me."

"Do you live here with your father?" the dirt mouth asked.

"Nope," the boy said. "Daddy died a couple of years ago. Got a sickness from the dirt or something. I don't remember much about it. Grandpa wouldn't let me go to the hospital to see him."

"Grandpa…is he Marcus Towers?"

"Yessir," little Marcus said. "Ever met him?"

The mouth didn't say anything for a moment. "Please, bring me some water."

The old Mexican ranch-hand saw the boy running up to the house and stopped his work on the old tractor. He told the boy he'd heard a shot and wondered if everything was fine. "*Si, si,*" Marcus said in a twangy Spanish. "*No mas era una tortuga,*" little Marcus told him. The old Mexican nodded and told him not to shoot too close to them. He'd seen a man, a long time ago, hurt because the shell of a snapping turtle shattered and sent tiny slivers into the man's leg, which got infected. "*No te preocupes,*" Marcus said and was inside the door. The old Mexican went back to his work and only looked up briefly when little Marcus ran out of the house with two canteens bouncing off his shoulder.

Marcus came back to the spot with two old canteens filled with tap water. When his shadow—longer still with the lowering of the sun—the stone eye focused on him. The boy's shadow was comforting. "Just pour it wherever you can," the dirt mouth told him.

Marcus opened the top of one of the canteens and let it stream down onto the dirt mouth and stone eye. A film of mud rolled over both the eye and mouth until Marcus could not see them. But, the ground drank the water and turned a dark brown. Soon, the eye emerged and the mouth formed again. "You want more?" Marcus asked it.

"Please," the mouth said and Marcus emptied the second canteen over it.

Just as with the first canteen, the mouth and eye vanished and reemerged, but as they did, the mud seemed to bubble and swell. The eye was no longer on flat ground, but raised as if on the edge of a sphere until the rising ball of mud took the mouth with it. The creature opened its mouth wide and gulped at the air, only to have the fringes of its lips turn dusty from the heat. "Can you bring me more?" it asked the boy. "I am very thirsty."

"I'd bet, laying out here in the sun all day long," little Marcus said. "But, I don't think I can. It's getting late and Grandpa is going to be coming home soon. He doesn't much like me wandering out here on my own."

"I understand," the one-eyed creature said. It looked out at the land for the first time and Marcus couldn't tell if water dripped from its eye or if the thing were crying. "Do you see those *nopales* over there?" it asked him.

"Yep," little Marcus said and spotted the green cactus.

"Could you cut a few plates from it," the creature said. "Just lay them near me."

"I guess so," little Marcus said. "It won't take but a minute."

The boy took his Bowie knife and cut a few pieces off the plant and let them fall. Like a hungry man with a fork, he speared the plates and took them to the creature. At first, he wondered what to do. He wouldn't put his foot to them and get a thorn himself and the plates were too stubborn to slide off on their own. At the sight of Marcus's confusion, the creature spoke. "You may throw them at me," the creature said. "As you proved with your gun, I'm sure I will not be hurt."

"If you say so," little Marcus said and flicked his knife at the creature. The four plates thudded against its face and a few thorns did stick to its cheeks. But, once the plates settled, they shriveled and browned slowly and the creature's head rose a little into a head, neck, and the tops of shoulders.

"Thank you, Marcus," the creature said.

"You want me to come back tomorrow? I hear it's going to be hot as hell," Marcus said and clapped his hand over his mouth. "Sorry, I ain't supposed to be cussing."

"I don't mind," the creature said. "Before you go, may I ask you something?"

"Sure," Marcus said. "What is it?"

"Why aren't you afraid of me?" the creature asked and let one muddy lid slide over its stone eye.

"Aw, hell," Marcus laughed. "There's scarier stuff out here than you. Once, I came up on a family of skunk-pigs and they chased me all the way to the house. Grandpa had to shoot at them before they turned around." With that, the boy turned to leave.

"Marcus," the creature said. "I think…I think…my name is… Edmundo."

"Well," Marcus said and made the motion of tipping his hat, "I'm pleased to meet you. I'm going to tell my Grandpa all about you."

Looking off into the land, stone eye glassy, the creature said, "I hope that you do." But, Marcus was too far to hear him.

Marcus Towers senior was a tall man with a thick walrus moustache which always carried paper-thin shreds of peanuts and crusty remnants of beer foam. Along with the thick smell of Delicado cigarettes that wafted into the house when he came in, the scent of cheap perfume followed him. At home, he cursed a bit about the heat and the drought, and washed his face in the sink. Amalia, the old Mexican's wife, had two plates of a fragrant guisado ready for him and little Marcus.

Usually at dinner, Towers was drunk and would say little, sometimes grunting a question about his grandson's day. But, that day, he was unusually talkative, discussing the goings on of San Casimiro. The library had burnt down two days ago and little Marcus nodded and asked about the fat librarian, who often called him a little pig and wouldn't let him check out any books that were on the upper floors. But, all the books were gone now. "It ain't no surprise," Towers said. "That city-slicker was crazy as can be for moving here in the first place. Old Tenerio, the fire chief, he said that damn place burnt up for hours and hours. Books make good kindling, I'd imagine." He looked across the table to his grandson and said, "So, old Jose told me you went out shooting today."

"Yessir," little Marcus told him. "I just went for a walk and shot at a turtle."

"Did you get 'im?" Towers asked.

"Nope," Marcus lied. "Well, I got him, but the shot was too far. Just glanced off that shell."

"I'd bet," Towers said. "I seen a turtle once, it got glanced by a damn semi. It went spinning like a top and I was sure it was dead. But, wouldn't you know it, that old turtle just got up and went on walking into the brush."

"You know, Grandpa," little Marcus said. "I did see something weird."

"Oh, yeah? And what was that," the old man said and forked more guisado into his mouth.

"I don't know," little Marcus said. "It was like…a mud man. I found it in the middle of the tank past the dump. It talked to me."

Towers was smiling and nodding. Little Marcus was not a stranger to telling lies at the table. Towers allowed it on account that life on a ranch for a boy of eleven was often a boring one. He'd met many a rancher who spent half their time in a world that was in their heads only coming out of it long enough to tell tales of it and return. "What did it say?"

"Well," the boy said, shifting in his seat. "It scared me at first. You don't expect to find something like that on a walk. But, I got to talking to it. It was mighty hot. So, it asked me to bring it some water."

"You didn't go wasting no good water on your childishness, did you?" Towers asked.

"No, sir," little Marcus said. "I just got it out of the tap. I gave it two canteens worth of water. And, wouldn't you know it, it drank it right up. It said thank you and everything."

"Oh, yeah," Towers said and nodded. "Did you say you're welcome?"

"Dang it!"

"Language, boy," Towers warned.

"Sorry, sir," little Marcus said. "I didn't say you're welcome. But, I did cut up some *nopales* and tossed them at that thing. It ate them right up. Just left the skin and the thorns."

"That sounds nice," Towers said. "Did your new friend have a name, or did you just go and call it mud man?"

"Well," little Marcus said. "At first, it didn't even know its name. All it said was that it could remember a lady and two little girls or something. But, after I gave it water and all that, it remembered."

"I've seen plenty of people go crazy from the heat," Towers said. "Hell, I saw a man once got so dizzy from the heat, he took his pistol and shot up into the trees to get him a dove. I'll be damned if he didn't get one, pick it up, and drink up the blood. Poor ol' guy was never the same after that. So, I reckon your mud man could forget his name, spending all that time in the heat."

"Bird blood? That's gross," little Marcus said. "But, he *did* remember his name. It was…Edmundo!"

Towers dropped his fork and stared at his grandson. "What did you say?"

"He said he was named Edmundo," little Marcus said.

"Boy, I'm done with all of your foolishness," Towers barked, his face flushing with anger. "You're done eating. Go wash up and get to bed."

"But, Grandpa, I'm still hungry," little Marcus said.

"Don't make me get the belt off the hook," Towers said and pointed behind the boy with his fork. An old belt dangled off a nail in the wall. Little Marcus shuddered at the thought of it. "Now, get to bed. And no more of your damn stories." Little Marcus grumbled and did as he was told. But, even after he was gone, Towers thought about what the boy had said. Edmundo. A lady and two girls. He could figure that the boy would choose the name on account of the ranch, but he wondered where he dreamt up the lady and the two girls. Towers sat and wondered, but even after he pushed the thoughts aside, the old man could not force himself to continue eating.

The day, like all the others, was scorching. Little Marcus hadn't been out of the house a minute before tiny wings of sweat were forming on his overalls. He took his shotgun out again and two more canteens of water to the dry tank, past the dump site and the hunched turkey vultures that hung around it. Their burn-victim faces followed the boy as he walked through the shadows they cast off the old telephone poles. Little Marcus paid them no mind, eager to see the mud man, Edmundo.

It had not moved from among the bricks. The mud man's shoulders were still above the ground, but his face had dried to the color of sand. The stone eye was half open and from its lips, tiny puffs of dust rose and disappeared. "Are you okay?" little Marcus asked as he made his way to it. The dusty lid opened a bit and the stone focused. With great effort, the mud man nodded. "Man, oh man, I bet you'd like some water," little Marcus said and poured some of the first canteen onto the mud man's head. At first, all the water did was wash away the creature's features as the dirt soaked up the liquid. But, once the stream stopped, the mud man's face reconstructed itself.

"Thank you, Marcus," the mud man said. "Could you please give me more?"

"Sure I can," little Marcus said and emptied the first canteen.

The mud man soaked it up until it shook. From the shaking, the creature grew taller, the space between its arm and ribs now visible.

"Wow," little Marcus said. "It's like I'm growing my own friend." With that, he opened the second canteen and dumped it on the mud man. As before, it took in the water and grew until it was able to pull a single arm free from the earth. It was a disfigured thing topped with two fingers and a thumb.

The mud man looked at the appendage in awe, flexing and relaxing the fingers. As would a man coming out of a long slumber, the mud man stretched the arm, hoping to extract the other, but all he did was tear off the other at the elbow. It would not grow.

"Did that hurt?" Marcus asked.

"About the same as getting shot in the face," the mud man said. "But, that didn't hurt either. I think you've got to have a body to feel…pain."

"Nuh-uh," Marcus said. "Anything can be in pain. I've seen it. Sometimes, at night, my house sounds like it's in pain and it ain't nothing but bricks and wood."

Still looking at its own arm, the mud man sighed. "Marcus, a moment ago, you called me a friend."

"So?"

"Do you really believe that?" the mud man asked. "That we are friends."

"Well, sure," Marcus replied and grinned. "I talk to you as much as I do anyone else. Plus, you didn't get sore when I shot you. If I did anything half that dumb at home, my Grandpa would whip me good."

The mud man looked up as if the sound of the word 'whipping' sparked something in him. "Marcus, if you are my friend," it said after a moment. "Please bring your grandfather to me. Please show me to him."

"Well," little Marcus said. "I already told him about you and he got mad about it. Sent me right to bed when I still had half my plate. He thinks I'm just telling stories."

"What if I made him believe you?" the mud man asked.

"How's that?" little Marcus asked.

"We would have to do something to prove I exist then," the mud man reasoned. "You said he is not here until the evening, correct?"

"Yep."

"What time?"

"Oh, I don't know…" Marcus said and looked up at the sun. "Not for hours. Bout eight, if I had to say."

"Then tell him, at midnight," the mud man said. "He will hear me. I will call him."

"Okay," Marcus said as he made his way back to the hill. "But, I'll warn you, Grandpa gets mighty upset when people wake him up."

"I will take my chances," the mud man said and waved. When Marcus was out of sight, the mud man took out its stone eye and put it on the palm of his hand and waited until a bird caught the glint and circled down to investigate. The mud man's hand shut like a bear-trap when the bird landed. In the sun, it feasted on the bird's blood.

That evening, Towers was in a foul mood. A new dancer, a Japanese girl named Fujiko, had refused to buy him another beer when one of her thick high-heels knocked his all over the front of his shirt. Even his underwear had been soaked through. He tried to force Manuel, the owner of Bare Back's, to get him another free of charge, but the stout man had just laughed. Towers even tried to weasel a private dance from Fujiko as compensation, but she pretended not to understand him. Grumbling, he left Bare Back's and found his truck in the dirt parking lot.

The drive did nothing to diminish his mood. If anything, it made him angrier.

Once at home, Towers glared across the table at his grandson.

"Grandpa," little Marcus said after a while.

Towers stopped sopping up beans with his tortilla and met the boy's eyes. "Yeah," he said.

"Um…I have a message for you," little Marcus said and averted his eyes. He'd seen his Grandpa in those moods before and knew to beware anything that might anger him further.

"Oh yeah? From who?" Towers asked. "Don't tell me that old bastard Brizuela's been out here bitching about my fences. I swear, me and Cazares are about to have enough of that little man and we got the dang luck of being on either side of him."

"No, Grandpa…from the mud man," little Marcus said. He winced when Towers dropped his utensils and narrowed his eyes at him.

"Boy, what the hell did I tell you about making up bullshit stories, especially that one."

"I'm not making up stories, Grandpa," Marcus said. "He told me he was going to prove it to you."

"Oh really," Towers said. "And how's he going to do that?"

"I don't know, he just said that at midnight you'd hear him," Marcus told him.

Towers stood up and nodded. "Is that a fact," he mumbled. When Marcus tried to follow his Grandpa with his eyes, the old man pointed down at the plate and told him to eat and not to mind what he was doing.

Marcus knew it was coming, so he shoveled as much food as he could into his mouth and swallowed. The clink of metal on metal chirped behind him. The sound of leather wrapping around an old fist. The first lick was loud and made little Marcus bite down on his lip else he would scream. Amalia turned from her cleaning, but did nothing. The second lick was a shower of pain, hitting the same spot as the first. He hated that his Grandpa's aim had only improved in his advancing years. The third curled over little Marcus's shoulder and caught him half on the back and half on the chest. The boy was crying then.

"I don't want any more of your nonsense, do you hear me?" Towers shouted.

Little Marcus nodded and wiped his tears with the back of his arm.

"Now, wash up and go to sleep before I whoop you some more," Towers ordered and pointed in the direction of the boy's room with his thumb. "I swear, your daddy must be spinning in his grave with what a little liar you are."

Marcus went into the bathroom and examined the marks. They were already risen and pink. When he touched them, he couldn't help but wince. He knew it was not a lie, that the mud man existed and spoke to him, but he was not dumb enough to press his Grandpa on it, not when he was that angry.

The mud man spread its arms—the bird's blood being enough to bring out the other—to the moonlight. The pale blue light over the trees and grass and the flutter of bats in the air made its dirt mouth a smile. The air was cool and balmy from being in the middle of a dry tank and with the bricks around him like apostles, the mud man opened his mouth as much as it would allow. It inhaled deeply, puffing out his chest, making tiny motes of dust fleck off of his appendages. The mud man did this until it was almost bent over backwards. The moon told the mud man it was midnight and the mud man finally let out a scream.

"Give me back my land!" the mud man yelled and the words were heavy and deep. In the moonlight, slumbering doves and flycatchers flashed out of the trees like bullets and far off, an egret squawked and took flight.

"Give me back my land! Give me back my land!" the mud man seethed, his stone eye glowing. "Give me back my land!"

Towers was in the middle of a dream, one where he was teaching Fujiko a lesson for knocking over his beer. In his dream, she was kind to him, willing to take him into the *monte* and let him tie her to a tree. Let him strip her and do what he would, when he would, and how he would. As he was about to tilt her head back, letting her glossed lips part in waiting, he woke up to a terrible screaming.

He looked over the door, to the old clock he had that sounded each hour with Texas bird calls. The mockingbird's call was sounding quietly. It was midnight.

Still partially drunk, Towers couldn't tell if the sound came from his window or from the sky itself. He put on a pair of pants and a shirt and looked out to the ranch. The moonlight illuminated the wings of birds and bats alike as they raced away from the land. The screaming came again, from the direction of the dump site. Towers couldn't make it out, but decided that he needed to find it. He took his old pistol from the nightstand, checked it, and flipped the safety off. He took a flashlight from the closet and went off into the ranch.

He did not hear little Marcus slip through the door behind him.

As Towers passed the dump site, the scream came again. "Give me back my land!" the voice said and it stopped Towers in his tracks. The voice was familiar, though he hadn't heard it in over five decades. "Give me back my land!" it called again. Gun raised, Towers slowly made his way to the tank the boy had talked about. "Give me back my land! Give me back my land!"

The closer Towers got, the more his gun shook.

He dropped it all together when he saw the thing in the middle of the lake and it saw him. The screaming ceased and like a dog poised to strike, the mud man put both hands on the ground and sneered at Towers. The old man picked up his gun and advanced, not caring if he recklessly went through the high grass. The mud man did not move, surrounded by bricks, bricks that Towers remembered selecting himself. "What are you?" Towers whispered and leveled his pistol.

"The better question is *who* am I," the mud man said. "Do you not know me, Marcus Towers!" Its torso shook as it tried to claw its way to the old man, but the ground held fast. "You know me Marcus Towers! You knew me as Edmundo Salazar! I gave you a job! I gave you my roof!"

Towers shot the mud man once in the shoulder, but all that did was break off a chunk of his body, which grew back. "I don't know what you're talking about," Towers said, though the way he trembled said otherwise.

"No!" the mud man raged. "You don't remember taking me to town, getting me drunk fifty years ago! You don't remember hitting me over the head with a hammer and tying bricks to my hands and feet! You don't remember throwing me here! And my family! Where are they now that you've stolen everything from them! Where, you bastard!" The mud man lifted a brick from the ground and lobbed it at the old man.

The brick hit the old man in the leg, forcing him to hop on one foot as he rubbed the spot. "I didn't do shit to your family! They left once I got the ranch!" Towers shot again, this time hitting the creature in the eye, but it too just grew back.

"Don't you see, old man!" the mud man screamed. "You killed me once and I can't be killed again! Shoot at me until the kick breaks your hand and I'll still be here, waiting for you!"

"Is that a fact," Towers said and moved back, out of the reach of the mud man's bricks. With distance on his side, Towers took his time aiming and took off the mud man's cheek before the pistol was out of ammunition. "I'll be back, Edmundo. Don't you doubt that."

Little Marcus couldn't believe it. He knew that his Grandpa was prone to violence, but he didn't think upon meeting the mud man that his grandfather would insult it and shoot it until his gun was empty. He hid in the bushes until his Grandpa was out of sight and followed him at a distance. If what the mud man said was true, he was even more afraid of his Grandpa than before, and he thought that bordered on outright fear as it was.

The next day, trucks with massive tanks of stinking water came to the ranch. Towers sent them over to the dry tank and told them to go take a break somewhere. He recommended Bare Back's in San Casimiro and told the men he could manage dumping water into a tank by himself. One of the men inquired what the statuesque construction in the tank was, but Towers pretended not to hear him and handed them twenty dollars apiece for whatever they liked.

The old man waited until they were gone before venturing out into the tank. He shaded the mud man and grinned down at him. "So, the boy was right. I don't know how you did it or what you are now, but you're old Edmundo," Towers said.

"Give me back my—"

"I hated taking orders from you then, you old Mex," Towers said. "But, I'll shut you up once and for all. If drowning you once did it for fifty years, let's see if this one will stick until after I'm long dead and buried." With that, old Towers climbed the small hill and moved to pull the lever of one of the tankards. As he tried, little Marcus came from behind one of the bushes, crying.

"Don't do it, Grandpa," he pleaded, but all he got for the effort was a sharp backhand.

"Get the hell outta here, boy," Towers said. "You don't need to see none of this." He pulled the first lever. The water cascaded from the first truck and the old man went to the next and the next, pulling their levers and watching the flood as it encased the tank before spilling into it. At first, the mud man just looked up with an eye filled with utter hate, but once the waters rushed to its waist, it thrashed as if in pain. It splashed the water about, trying to save itself, but as it struggled, its fingers began to fall off one by one. Then an arm dropped off. It screamed up at them. For the old man, it was the scream of a bitter enemy promising to meet again, gun in hand. For the boy, it was the scream of a scared man desperate to be free of his second death. Soon, the water rushed over the creatures head, and neither of them could tell if the bubbling was from the mud man or the gallons and gallons of water flooding the tank.

The torrents slowed to trickles and then stopped. The tank was not half full, but full enough to cover the mud man and let his body dissipate throughout, never to be whole again. Towers looked out at the water glistening in the sun and laughed and took out his pistol and shot the water. When his clip was empty, he felt a lancing pain on his leg and yelped.

He turned to see little Marcus, Bowie knife out in front of him like a tiny sword. "Why did you have to do that, Grandpa! Why! He didn't do nothing to you," the little boy hollered.

"Boy," Towers said, checking his buttocks for blood and turning his back to the lake. "You best give me that knife and take your whipping."

Little Marcus stepped back, his knife shaking. "Or what? Are you going to kill me too! Just like you did to Edmundo…twice!"

"Boy, don't fool with me," the old man said and advanced a step, but the sound of gurgling water stopped him. As he turned to the tank, it felt as though the earth beneath his feet were shifting, being pulled from under him. The three trucks buckled and rolled into the tank, half submerging like metallic pigs. From the center of the tank, the water seemed to boil, but no steam came forth, just an eye the size of a dinner table. Like a sea god, the mud man rose past the waters so that it seemed as though the tank cemented it to this world. Old Towers nearly folded from the weight of the eye.

"Run, little Marcus," the mud man said. "As the rightful owner, I give this place to you. Go and live well. After today, I will bother this land no more." The creature waited until the boy was running before it brought down both arms beside Towers, knocking him off balance. The old man pleaded with the towering monolith, begging not to be drowned as he had done to him. That made the mud man chuckle, sending stone sized chunks of mud off his body like fleas. "No," the mud man said. "I will not drown you, as you did me. I am not a monster." It lifted up one hand and let Towers watch the mud slowly run down the appendage. "This will be more like being buried alive," the creature admitted and slammed its fist down on the old man.

Like a coffin of clay, it closed around him, filling his nose and flowing down his screaming throat until his lungs were filled with it. Until the land itself squashed his terror.

—ETC.—

Sins of the Father

When Pop said it the first time, I laughed at him. When he said it to that old gypsy, Madam Zerkow, I couldn't help it. I took him to the annual *feria* to take in the sights, the smells. Let him torture other people for a change. I wheeled his old, fat ass up and down the dirt lot, from tent to tent. Until we got to that fortune teller, that Mexican wish granter, I thought the old man was asleep, making me push his invalid ass all through the broken fairgrounds for nothing. "Let's go in there, Bud," he rasped at me underneath the crystal ball banner set up outside her tent.

Then, there we were. In front of some saggy breasted harridan waving her wrinkled hands over an electric crystal ball. She went through the motions, touching the sides of her graying head like she was holding council with the spirits. After telling Pop not to speed on the highway and to beware blonde women who seem too eager for his affection, she asked if he had a wish. Some desire to beg from the universe. "I never want to die," he spat and followed the wish with a long stream of wet, hacking coughs that covered the sound of me giggling. "I want to live forever."

"That is…a very big wish," Madam Zerkow replied, rubbing her fuzzy chin.

"I never want to die," Pop said again.

"C'mon, Pop, let's go," I told him.

"It is…a very big wish…"

He flopped his dead hands up at mine. "Bud, pay the woman what you got," he said and made puppet gestures.

"Pop, that's all the money I brought," I said and started pulling him away.

Pop threw a fit. Shaking in his seat, moving that flab like a pendulum from side to side. If it wasn't for me, his dumb ass would have capsized like so much flesh into a big, useless puddle. "God damn it, son! Pay the woman!" he yelled. "After all I've done for you, you ol' son of a bitch. Ingrate. Pay the damn woman her money. I got a big wish, damn it."

"Pop--"

"You'll do as I say!" he roared and covered his mouth to release another series of coughs.

All the while, the gypsy was just watching us, calmly wondering if she was going to weasel us out of a couple of bucks.

Pop dangled one hand frantically and I fished out thirty bucks from my wallet and gave them to her.

"I will consult with the spirits, *senor*," she said and slid the money into a tattered, purple fanny-pack at her hip.

"Thank the damn woman!" Pop ordered.

"I thank you, miss," I said and got him out of there. With no money left, I decided to go back to the truck.

"You heard that, didn't you, boy?" he coughed at me without so much as turning. "I ain't going to die, now. I'm going to be here longer still and my worthless son was bitchin' about putting up a lousy thirty dollars to make sure I live a full life. After all I spent on you. You know how many diapers I bought you? How much those fuckin' braces cost? Like you care. Cursed is the man with a son like mine," he kept on and I wondered how long he'd survive if I left him at the damn *feria*. The coyotes would have get to him eventually.

*   *   *

It wasn't a month later he died of a stroke right there at the dinner table. I thought he'd choked on the chicken pot-pie on account of him dancing in his chair like a dying fish, the food kind of pushing out of his mouth like a chewed up slug. He shook and trembled, and I watched him same as I would a bit of magic or a miracle. Seeing him struggling, I imagined it all. The rest of my life in a second. The silent years I'd have with anyone or no one. My choice. The TV I'd get to watch at any damn time of day. The Sunday mornings I'd sleep through without having to change his catheter and wiggle him into a snug suit for church. The pills I'd never have to count. The mush I'd never have to spoon feed him again. I saw it all when he went limp.

I kept on eating.

It was the best meal I ever had. Nothing but a microwaveable pot-pie, but then, it tasted like youth. I cleared the table, washed the plates, put them back in the cabinets, and grabbed a beer. It was my house now and I'd drink on Sunday if I damn well pleased.

I went back into the dining room and he was moving again.

"Shit," I said and put down the beer. "Well, at least I didn't call nobody to come and get you," I told him as I went and wiped the chewed food off his chin and bib. Just like him, I thought. Giving me a little damn hope, a little satisfaction, only to go and take it away by being a stubborn old ox.

The days went by with him a little different, but the same. He couldn't talk but in short moaned sentences. I was happy he wasn't as yappy as he used to be. No 'hands out of yer pockets, boy.' No 'I shoulda shot you in the delivery room, boy.' A few days later, he started stinking. Not just the smell of an old man covered in bed sores with a decade's worth of shit stuck in his ass, but a real stink. The kind of stink you only run into on hot highways where a skunk had its head splattered and the buzzards hadn't gotten to it yet. He was turning green and his veins were getting black.

The next day, he tried to bite me. Like a mantis, he hooked my arm and opened his mouth wide, but I was faster.

"The hell's the matter with you!" I yelled, but he wasn't looking at me, just my naked arm.

"Hungry…" he pleaded and tried to move. "So…hungry." He threw a shaky leg out of his chair and I didn't stop him. He'd tried standing on pure stubbornness before.

"Pop, you're just going to give me more work to do," I said. "But, go on. See what happens to you."

He kicked out the other leg and steadied himself on the chair. It took him a while, but he did it. Joints creaking like dry branches, he rose defiantly and took one shaky step to me. Then another. "Meat…" he moaned. "Bring me…meat…"

I went to sit him in his chair, but he tried to bite me again. I shoved him to the floor and for a second, I thought I'd really killed him. I stood watching, waiting to see what he would do. Beetle-like, he started moving, calling for meat. "Fine, you old bastard, I'll get you something."

I went to the butcher and got a few ounces of everything. Pork, lamb, beef, poultry, fish, goat. Everything. He tried them all and vomited them up onto himself.

"Fresh…meat…" he managed, slowly inching toward my hand, his mouth opening to show his dozen yellow teeth. "Blood…" he groaned.

"Damn it, you smelly bastard, I'll hunt you something up," I cursed at him and went out. "*Shit*, even dead, that old fat ass is still bossing me around."

*　　*　　*

I went down to Rosita's and had a drink. Sizing people up. The *vaqueros* were no good. They were all too weary of me and Pop and his stream of slurs. He'd called them a bunch of wetbacks even when they'd helped him into the truck after church. I didn't want it to be a woman. If I hadn't had one since the county stuck me with the old man, I sure as shit wasn't about to go giving him one to have his way with. I sat there wondering, watching, waiting.

Allen Serrato came in around midnight. He was the biggest man in the county and one of the scummiest. No one would miss him. Hell, some people might thank me. Allen was a thief and addict with a famous right cross, the haymaker. He got a beer and found a table to himself.

"Hey Allen," I said as I went up to his table.

"Hey, Bud. How's it hanging," he told me.

"It's hanging," I replied. "You mind if I sit? I got to talk to you about something."

"You ain't going to accuse me of stealing nothing from you, now are you? I don't take kindly to it," he said, showing me his fist.

"No, nothing like that."

"Then sit," he said and motioned with the haymaker.

I did.

"What did you need?"

"Well," I said and looked around, hamming up my nerves. "You remember my old man?"

"Yeah, the warhorse," he laughed. "How is the old son of a bitch? I haven't seen him for about two months."

"There's a reason for that," I whispered. "He died a month ago."

"Sorry to hear that," he told me. "What's that got to do with me, though?"

"I didn't tell anyone," I said.

"Why not? Isn't that something people generally like to know?"

"Well, I've been cashing his social security checks," I lied. "I've cashed two and I don't see why I've got to stop."

"Maybe because he's dead," Allen told me.

"The county doesn't know that, but they will. I got a call today that they're sending up an inspector to see how Pop is. I need to get rid of him."

"You still got the body?" he gasped in a whisper.

"Yeah, what the hell was I supposed to do? He weighs over two-hundred and some. I couldn't bury him alone," I told him. "But, you, you're big. That's what I wanted to ask you about. Help me."

"I don't know…"

"I'll give you half of the check every month," I told him. "A hundred and fifty bucks every month for a year. C'mon. Don't pretend like you couldn't use it. That's…," I did the math, "eighteen hundred bucks for one night's work."

He thought about it, drank his beer, and said, "Let's kick this pig then."

Neither of us said much on the ride over. There was nothing to say, really.

At the house, Allen had to light a cigarette to fight off the smell. "God damn," he spat. "You'd think with all that extra money, you'd buy some air freshener or a box of baking soda or something."

"He's in back," I said and pointed. We found the room and stood there looking at the old man. He'd managed to get to the corner and sat there like wounded soldier shot stone dead, hands and legs splayed out. "You get him into the chair," I told Allen and went to get the seat ready.

Allen stood inspecting Pop's face, the gangrene color of his leather skin. "Bud, you better not fuck me on even one of those checks."

"I won't."

"He ain't going to split, is he?"

"Split?"

"Yeah," Allen said. "Split. I know drowners can get so loose in their skin that they'll split and bust open the second you try to move them."

"He didn't drown, Allen," I said. "He had a stroke or something. Pick him up so we can wheel him to the truck."

"Fine," Allen sighed. "You're the man with the money." He bent over to wrap his arm around Pop, whispering, "God, he stinks." Allen didn't notice the old man's eyes opening.

Pops bit down on him hard.

Allen tried screaming, but the old man was punching his five bottom teeth into Allen's throat. Like a dumb ape, Pop hugged the twitching body in his useless arms and ate. After a while, Allen stopped twitching. Wet, piggish chomps filled the room as Pop went at all the meat and bones, his tired jaws stronger than ever before. His cataract covered eyes stared at me as he gummed strips of Allen's scalp. "More…" he moaned at me with skin stuck to his teeth.

"Don't you start getting greedy with me, Pop," I spat. "You'll get what I give you."

I closed the door and locked it from the outside, grumbling about the worst thirty dollars I ever spent.

The "Paletero Murders"

I.

Case #: 1798-191.3
Transcript: Manolo Andrade
Interviewing Officer: Sheriff Claudio Reynoso
Interview #: 6

[Mr. Andrade entered the San Casimiro Sheriff's Department at 9:45 a.m. Mr. Andrade claimed to have information regarding case # 1798-191.3]

"Please do not think I knew her well because I didn't. That Dolores. I had seen her many times sitting on her porch, fanning herself. I did not always live here, you see. Selling paletas was not my first profession. I sell them on the street. You, Sheriff Reynoso, you have seen me selling paletas. I remember you had a… strawberry flavored paleta last week, yes? I knew it. Despite my boring job, I've kept my memory.

"I have a good memory for things, Sheriff. I always have. If I had a moment to think, I could tell you what every person has ordered from me this week. Even the people passing through. The mayor, he likes pineapple. Gets three every time I stop at his office, and I don't think he gives any to his kids. They're all for him, the *marano*.

"Oh...I'm sorry. I meant that *he*...eh...not you, officer... but...

"Yes, I am sorry. Dolores. Well, when I first started with my cart, I went through the whole town. Border to border. It sounds like a lot of walking, but you can do it in an hour. Less if you don't have any customers. That's what I liked about San Casimiro at first. The walks. Here, the scenery is nice. It is colorful. The trees. They are old. Give good shade. But, I keep rambling. Some other workers—ditch diggers and caballeros—we used to talk at Rosita's some nights. They told me never to go down the dirt road past Callahan. 'But, there are houses there, aren't there? Some *vaqueros* wouldn't mind a paleta,' I told them.

"'But, Manolo,' they said, 'some of the others, they went there once. They thought the same as you. And, *chinga*, we never saw them again.'

"'You know *la migra* picks us up once in a while. They do it when they come up for review,' I said. Honestly, I thought they were kidding with me. I was new, after all.

"'*Pendejo*, I don't know where you were before, but San Casimiro is different. *La migra* hasn't come here in years. It's not that. I heard there's a *bruja* living out there. Selling fifty cents of flavored shit and risking my soul for it? You're crazy if you go there.'

"I thought they were trying to frighten me. People like to play tricks on others. A witch. Could you imagine hearing such a thing? From the old ladies, I could understand. They like to blame things they don't understand on ghosts and other things. But, not the young. Yes, they listen to the stories, but they never believe them.

"*Pero*, let me get on with it. I went out to Callahan. Went through the whole block and ended up at the dirt road. I'm embarrassed to admit it, but I must have passed that road ten times, my bell jingling softly. I don't believe in witches or black magic, but when you hear not to do something so many times...well, sometimes you listen.

"But, I told myself, *Manolo, you are a grown man. There is no such thing as a witch.*

"There were a few houses down the road, but I don't think anyone else lived down there. Oh, no one else did? That would explain it, I guess. You don't just have a yard full of paleta carts and not have anyone notice."

II.

Case #: 1798-191.3
Transcript: Dolores Guarecuco
Interviewing Officer: Sheriff Claudio Reynoso
Interview #: 1

[Ms. Guarecuco was detained after Jaime Raz, a local paleta vendor presumed missing since July 9th, ran from Ms. Guarecuco's home, hands and mouth bound in duct tape. Mr. Raz was found at the 300 block of Callahan Road, nude, emaciated, and incoherent. Mr. Raz indicated Ms. Guarecuco as his kidnapper citing numerous counts of aggravated sexual assault. Patrol Unit 3 responded at 12:27 p.m. Ms. Guarecuco entered the San Casimiro Sheriff's Department at 12:45 p.m.]

"He loved me, you know. Jaime. He used to come by my house four or five times a day, ringing his bell for me to hear. He said I was his best customer. I told him he was taking advantage of me, but that I didn't mind. Not with such a cute salesman.

"Yes, you said that already.

"I understand my rights and I don't want a lawyer. I've done nothing wrong. Jaime loves me, he said so himself. He's just playing hard to get like a little schoolboy. Otherwise, he wouldn't have said all those sweet things to me.

"Oh, I'll tell you. Jaime came by my porch. It was the third time that day and it was *hot*.

"'Ms. Dolores,' he said. When he said my name, I'll

tell you, I was in heaven. 'Ms. Dolores,' he said, 'paletas go great with pretty girls and warm weather.' He was already reaching in his cart, even though I didn't say anything. He liked to surprise me with a new flavor every day. He'd hold it behind his back and put out his hand. Once, he even got on one knee to give it to me. I just couldn't resist his charms. I know, mother said to never settle for someone lower than you, but with Jaime, I couldn't help myself.

"The others? No, they're different. Jaime's different. He loves me. I knew it the day he came to my house and reached into his cart. He called me Ms. Dolores and said, 'Paletas go great with pretty girls and hot weather.'

"I told him, 'Jaime, you're just trying to take advantage of my romantic nature.' But, I was always ready with my money. I kept it in a box where I could reach it quick. Just as soon as I heard Jaime ringing his bell. As you can see, I can't move around much, and I didn't want Jaime to have to wait in the sun.

"And, do you know what my Jaime did? When I gave him my money, he took my hand and said, 'Ms. Dolores, when I try to take advantage of your kind heart, you'll know it.'

"That's what he said last time. Just like that"

[Ms. Guarecuco remained silent temporarily.]

"Jaime loves me. He's just playing hard to get. You'll see. All of them loved me. Every single one."

III.

Case #: 1798-191.3
Transcript: Jaime Raz
Interviewing Officer: Sheriff Claudio Reynoso
Interview #: 2

[Mr. Raz was treated at the San Casimiro County Clinic

for dehydration, minor lacerations to his hands and knees, and numerous bite marks around his lips, nose, ears, and genitalia. Upon release, the San Casimiro Sheriff's Department requested his presence for a formal accusation. Mr. Raz entered headquarters at 9:14 a.m.]

"That crazy bitch. She said that? That I held her hand and told her I loved her? That I called her beautiful? I swear, I thought any jackass could see through that. A little flirting is another pound of *fajita* if you know what I mean. I tell that shit to everyone. The *viejitas*, the *gordas*, even the *jotos*. Whatever to sell more.

"Be nice to the customer, they buy more. It's simple. Give them what they want to get what you want.

"I can't believe she said that? She said that I would pass by all the time. Well, of course I did. Have you seen her? She fills the damn porch. I don't know how that *gorda* hasn't flattened her damn rocking chair. *Como una bestia!*

"I'm no catch, Sheriff. I know that. But, come on.

"No, I don't remember exactly how long I went by her house like that. Maybe two weeks. Maybe a little more. Hell, what else was I supposed to do before the schools let out or the *vaqueros* come back into town for a steak? Wait on the side of the highway and pray? I made good money off her. And how does she treat me, tries to fucking eat me.

"She's guilty as sin. Lock her up. And once I'm done with all this, I'm getting the hell out of this town. I'd rather dig ditches until I'm an old man than stay in the town that bred Dolores Guarecuco."

IV.

Case #: 1798-191.3
Transcript: Katarina Ochoa
Interviewing Officer: Sheriff Claudio Reynoso
Interview #: 7

[Independently, Mrs. Ochoa contacted the San Casimiro Sheriff's Department offering information on case # 1798-191.3]

"No, I don't know Dolores personally. I met her once. Imagine that, once the whole time she lived near Callahan. Not even half a mile from us. She wouldn't leave home, that Dolores.

"What's that? Oh, no. I never saw her do anything strange. I never saw her *do* anything. Never once at the general store. Never at Rosita's. Never even at church, if you can imagine that.

"I heard Anita, you know, Mr. Palacio's girl, she used to deliver groceries over there on account of Dolores being so...you know...*big*. She could hardly check the mail without help.

"Her momma was that way, too. Very large women in that family. But, I don't remember her looking that way as a girl. When her mother died, I think that's when she started. It couldn't have been easy, but I can't have imagined it would have led her to *this*.

"Never in my wildest dreams.

"But, like I said, it wasn't *her* that I thought was odd. It was the *paleteros*. At first, you hear the bell and maybe go to the window to see, but I never much did. Sweets are an indulgence I hardly partake in. But, one day about three months ago, there was one man. He was stoop-shouldered *viejo* with a white, white moustache.

"I was watering the yard. Please don't say anything, Sheriff. I know the county's in a drought, but you've seen my flowers. They're too precious to dry-out.

"But, the man's name was Cesar something. 'Is it tough pushing that cart in the heat?' I asked him once.

"He smiled and told me, '*Senorita*, I get to put my arm in a freezer all day.' He reached into the cart and handed me one. 'I'm the one who gets to feel sorry for the world,' he told me. Cesar was very nice.

"Yes, he'd go down Dolores's way. I don't know how it happened, but time just flew by. You lose track of people. I saw him a few times after that, but then, he just stopped coming by. I still heard the bell ringing now and again, so, I figured Cesar was still selling paletas.

"It took me a good month to look out the window and find out it was someone else."

V.

Case #: 1798-191.3
Transcript: Deputy Sheriff Jay Sutton
Interviewing Officer: Sheriff Claudio Reynoso
Interview #: 3

[Deputy Sheriff Sutton and Deputy Sheriff Egan were first to arrive at Ms. Guarecuco's residence. Once there was no answer at the door, weapons were drawn. Upon entering the house, they met no resistance until Ms. Guarecuco was discovered in her backyard, attempting to flee the scene.]

"I'd never seen anything like it. Never. There must've been thirty carts in that yard. Even an ice cream truck. I even remembered it. You know, Claudio, the one with Lucky Luke on it. Man, who knows how long they'd been there. A bunch had weeds growing through them. A whole lot of rust. Hell, one of those carts had a baby mesquite coming out the middle of it.

"And there she was, moving like a penguin. I let Egan get her. It wasn't like she was getting far.

"The inside though, that was something to see. Bones. There were bones covering the table, all clean. And I mean 'the-ants-got-at-it' clean. All stacked up like towers.

"Fucking paleta wrappers everywhere. I mean, you heard my boots coming a mile away. They're still sticky from walking through Dolores's house, and that's that I hosed them down once the lab guys were done with them.

"I mean, shit, I knew she wasn't all there. Had to

pass by there once on account of a lot of anthills or something. Illegal dumping or a dead dog. You know Old Lady Ochoa and her binoculars. She pretends not to be in anyone's business, but she's knee deep in it. Just you wait, one day, there'll be a big tell-all, like in Hollywood, except it'll be about this little shit town, and right under the title, we'll see Katarina Ochoa, Lead Chronicler.

"Those ants were big suckers too, I'll tell you. Fire ants that'll climb right up you and go for your mouth. I've seen it. Old ranch-hand my uncle knew. I won't get into it.

"There were a bunch of anthills around her property. You could see whole bugs getting pulled in from the *monte*. I mean, those ants must've been spread out an acre. And there was Dolores, watching me give a walk around the front of her place. Trying to give me the eyes behind those pudgy fingers. No thank you! Shit, being the stranger in a strange land around here makes it a little tough, but not that tough. Hell, after I gave the walk around, I just called Palos, the exterminator.

"But, come to think of it, when I drove off, I did see a paletero walking down that way. Gave him a wave and kept on driving. I wonder if he's one of those we found."

VI.

Case #: 1798-191.3
Transcript: Candelario Palos
Interviewing Officer: Sheriff Claudio Reynoso
Interview #: 4

[In March, Mr. Palos, a local exterminator, was called to the residence of Ms. Escontrias to deal with growing fire-ant colonies. It should be noted that the residence of Dolores Guarecuco is located half a block east of the Escontrias residence. Mr.Palos arrived at the San Casimiro Sheriff's Department for questioning at 11:21 a.m. Mr. Palos was visibly intoxicated.]

"Duct tape, brother. Duct tape. That's the most important thing I take with me for a job. See, when you go out there on these ranch calls, no telling what kind of nasty you're going to run into. Seems like shit around here just goes wild. I used to run this business near San An, and they were tame as can be compared to here. Over there, those city folk get an itty-bitty wasps' nest—two or three suckers tops—and they ran to the phone. Hid their children. And, if they didn't, nine times out of ten, they didn't grow up in a big city.

"But, San Casimiro, that's a different monster all together. You got to put on the long sleeves, the gloves, tie up your face, get those goggles on, and even then, you still need more.

"Know what you need?

"You got it, duct tape.

"I knew a guy that went to kill a hive of bees, and wouldn't you know it, they crawled into his gloves, down his shirt. He got stung round forty different times. Was picking those stingers out like he was popping pimples. Ants, bees, hornets, hell, all of them, you give them an opening and they'll go ahead a fuck you.

"Brother, those things just think different. When push comes to shove, they don't worry about little Timmy back home or how much the wife is going to miss them. Fuck no. They go out there like tiny sam-u-rais. They want to die for the big picture. They don't think, they just do. That's how they've gotten along for millions of years. Did you know other than their size, most bugs haven't evolved in a billion years? No joke. And you see it here, not like in other places.

"Middle of nowhere Texas, it's like hell cut open and shit's crawling out little by little. Don't believe me? Hell, I told you about them city folk. See a little sugar ant trail in the kitchen and you've got to talk them out of burning down the fucking house. And that was common. Common as all hell.

"Now, the weirdest call I ever got here was a nest

of hornets that came with some hellish stink. I mean it made you tear up, you hear me? You see, they'd carved out a nice little nest in some dead, bloated hog. The whole gut was split open like someone cut it with a knife. Even with the duct tape, I wouldn't have been able to kill half of them. Too much ground to cover even if I was going in there like Eastwood, two guns blazing. There would have been hornets jumping out of the eyes, the ears, straight out the ass to get a whack at me. And hornets, they'll sting you until they're just running on fumes and you been dead an hour.

"I ended up having to set that pig on fucking fire. Now, that was cool. Something I sure as shit couldn't have done in the city. Hell, this guy even had a torch ready. Kept it around for pear burning, like the damn drought would give him the chance. But, I'll be damned if I didn't strap that son of a bitch on and go to work. Lit that pig up. Those hornets came flying out of there, their wings and legs catching on fire. Looked like a big battleship letting loose with every gun. Fucking fireworks, brother. Fireworks.

"Oh, yeah. The Guarecuco house was a strange one too. Did you know, you find an ant hill, it'll lead you to every dead animal and trash within a mile. Just got to follow the thread like that guy with the man-bull, you know what I'm talking about? What's his name…

"Yeah, that guy, Theseus. But, when I got to the Guarecuco house, I'll tell you, I knew it wasn't going to be an easy job.

"Fucking anthills two feet high. Must've been six or seven hills all around. One was so big I thought I was a pile of clay pressed up against one of those abandoned sheds, but the second they felt me coming, those red bastards came out in force. Had to hop around like the Oklahoma kid just to save my ankles. I went to the truck, got out my canister of Boric acid. Funny stuff, that acid. It sucks up all the water in those little suckers. Like salt on a slug, just shrivels them up until all you have is a bunch of dead little raisins. Problem is, most times, you kill them, more ants come around collecting the dead ones. Naturally, I don't say any of that to my customers.

Doubt they'd like to know Boric acid keeps me coming by for three months, spraying and respraying.

"I got three of those hills done before that Guarecuco woman comes shambling off her porch. I heard her before I saw her. Those steps, I tell you, sounded like they were going to snap. She tells me that I don't need to do all of them. The ones by her house aren't bothering her.

"'Miss,' I say to her. 'Unless you get them all, the problem won't stop. Sure, there probably won't be that many on account of a fourth of them being dead, but a million ants are still a million ants.' And do you know what she tells me? She tells me the ants help clean up her yard. Like they were little gnomes that cut her damn grass and watered the trees. I couldn't see into the backyard, mind you. She had a couple of old ash trees that just hung there, dead for a decade, and some old ivies that netted between them. The anthills were spilling out from the busted fences.

"'Miss,' I told her again. 'If I don't work this, don't get them all, I won't be able to call it finished. Killing a few ants just to come back in a week to do it again just doesn't seem right to me.'

"What she do then? I'll be damned if she didn't wait a minute and take a swing at me with her cane. Well, a rusty pipe if you want to split hairs. But, she swung at me all the same. I told her to calm down, but she just kept swinging. If I hadn't've spritzed that Boric acid at her big feet, she'd probably be trying to bust my head open still."

VII.

Case #: 1798-191.3
Transcript: Dolores Guarecuco
Interviewing Officer: Sheriff Claudio Reynoso
Interview #: 1

"About who? Jose Manrique. I don't know that man. I've never met him!

"Oh, that was his name? Yes, but I never knew him by that name. Just as the Guero. There is not much to tell, really. He came by my house many times, always jingling his bell like all the rest. I bought many paletas from him. How could I resist? He tipped his hat to me every day and winked. Never gave me the chance to get off my chair to buy one. No, no. My Guero, he knew I don't move too good. He knew me very well.

"He would come up to my porch and sit with me, eating a paleta himself. The Guero was very kind to me. And the more he passed my door, the more I knew he loved me. Why else would he bother me so? There's a whole town to sell candy to. But, even on days that I knew no paletero was about, he would come to my home and sit with me. He was very kind.

"No, I don't want to look at those pictures. I know what he looked like, and I'll never forget that.

"I said I won't look at them. I don't care where you found him or how you found him. I remember well enough. He…he came to house on a Sunday. Neither of us went to church. He believed in nothing, and I couldn't manage to get to church on time if I wanted to, not unless I started walking the night before. But, he came to me not just with paletas, but with real food. Styrofoam boxes filled with fajita plates from Rosita's and bunuellos and chamoy. I did not want to take him inside. I can't clean very well in my condition, and my disability check can't cover a maid.

"The Guero could always convince me to do anything. I took him inside. He cleaned a space on the table and we ate like two normal people. I hadn't eaten like that…well, ever. When momma was around, eating was what she did all day long. Always a bit of this or that in one hand and a paper fan in the other. But, there we sat, the Guero and me, eating like normal people. We finished the fajita and went for the buneullos at the same time. Ay, when our fingers touched, I know he pulled away, but he was always so bashful. He smiled and looked away, but I couldn't. Not after that.

"I watched him eat and wipe his mouth and lick his

fingers. That's when I walked over to him. He took me in his arms and we kissed for the first time. It was all such a blur. We kissed and before I knew it, we were on the ground, wrestling with one another. He was the first man I'd ever been with, and I was happy because I knew he loved me.

"What? I don't care what the evidence says. Your doctors don't know the truth. I didn't fall on top of him, he pulled me onto him. I didn't pin him to the ground. He held me there. So, he could have gotten broken ribs from anywhere. San Casimiro is a tough town. Is it because of my size? Is that why it makes more sense for me to have pinned him to the ground and suffocated him? Is it so hard to think a man could love a woman like me, Sheriff? No, I don't know how to explain the bite marks. When he was making love to me, he nibbled on me, and I did the same to him. I was a virgin. I thought that was how it was done.

"No, he wasn't the only paletero to love me. There were…many."

VIII.

Case #: 1798-191.3
Transcript: Manolo Andrade
Interviewing Officer: Sheriff Claudio Reynoso
Interview #: 6

"It was by chance that I was in that neighborhood. You know Marco Escontrias? Yes, the butcher. He invited me to his little *ranchito* for his birthday. We spent the whole night drinking and dancing. We weren't many there. A half dozen men and their wives, but it was a good time. And, I'm sure this has happened to you, Sheriff, but I had a bit too much tequila.

"Marco, though, is a good man. He knew how dangerous it was to walk the *monte* in the middle of the night, drunk as I was. So, he let me sleep in one of the trucks parked outside. I didn't sleep very well, mind you. Those little single cabs are horrible on your back. There's no place for your head and you've got to deal with three different buckles digging into your sides all night. But, anyway, I guess that's why I didn't sleep too well.

"I woke with the sun and started walking. My apartment is not so far from there. I still needed my cart for the day, after all. The mornings here, they are truly something. The smell of wet grass fresh on the breeze. The cool wind that sticks your shirt to your body. The birds...they were nice too. As colorful as the sky. And the only way to warm up is to move, move, move.

"And I saw a bird, a strange bird for the morning. It was a buzzard. One of the kinds with the burnt flesh faces. What do you call them?

"Yes, a turkey vulture. You are very knowledgeable, Sheriff.

"I saw it flying, but not very high up. It was not searching for anything, it was flying away from something, like my approach had scared it away. Now, Sheriff, please don't think me a nosy person. I'm not. Where I come from, you mind your business or you end up dead. But, I suppose the tequila was still in my head, and I wanted to see what was dead.

"It led me to the side of Guarecuco's backyard. You've seen it, the trees are thick around it, and the grass had been left to run wild.

"It's no surprise. If Dolores couldn't move to the street to get a paleta from me, how could she get onto a lawnmower, let alone push one through that jungle. I don't like to admit this, Sheriff, but I was curious. San Casimiro isn't very big. After a month, I knew almost everyone except for Dolores and a few others.

"I got close to the fence and moved some of the leaves away and...well, *chinga*, that smell nearly made me vomit. I turned around to get the awful stink out of my nose and started coughing. I guess that's what woke her up because pretty soon, Dolores was at one of her windows, sticking half her body out the window like she was stuck. Swore she'd get a shotgun and I'm not in the habit of calling a bluff like that.

"But, what I saw, the little I saw...that was enough

for me to know the guys weren't just telling me
stories about the other paleteros. In that yard, I
don't know how many carts were in there. Some turned
over, missing wheels. Others you could only see the
bells full of webs that rang in the breeze like wind
chimes. Others moved like some *tlaquache* had made a
home in there. *Pero*, the weirdest thing was a rusty
old truck. An ice cream truck. The sides all faded
from the sun and the rains. But, like I said, I didn't
wait around to see if she really had a shotgun or if
she really was stuck in the window. Where I come from,
you don't go sticking your nose into the business of
others, no matter how crazy you think they are."

IX.

Case #: 1798-191.3
Transcript: Katarina Ochoa
Interviewing Officer: Sheriff Claudio Reynoso
Interview #: 7

"If you ask me, how couldn't we have seen it before?
It's so clear. Sheriff, you've lived here as long as
the rest of us. You must have been a boy, but you
remember the Guarecucos. You couldn't miss them.

"Poor Viviana, what that horrible man—God curse
his wicked soul—put her through. I'll never forget it,
not in all my life. That Giraldo took that *puta*, Ms.
Valencia—God rest her—to the drive-in movies. Right
there in front of the whole town. I got so mad, I
screamed at my date and didn't even know why. It was
infuriating. There he was, Mr. Guarecuco holding a bag
of popcorn and another woman's hand. But, it wasn't
even that. The looks they got were the worst part.
They are a sin on the soul of this town.

"What was so bad about them? They didn't exist!
Not one person, not Jim the cashier, not Lupe the
attendant, not even the kids Dolores's age batted an

eyelash at the sight of that man carrying on outside his marriage. It's ungodly!

"She may not have been the prettiest or the smartest, but she didn't deserve *that*. He drove her to do that to herself.

"Don't pretend you didn't see the bruises on her eyes less the bigger she got. Like the bigger she got, the less that *bruto* beat her. I don't even want to think of what he might have done to Dolores, that poor girl.

"My mother used to tell me about what Viviana would say at their sewing circle. Giraldo was out all hours, with all kinds of people. Came home drunk every night and had her like she was some sow. And she'd just eat and eat, tell her stories, and eat and eat. That poor woman could hardly use her needles she got so big. You ask me, that woman was putting on a pound for every bit of hurt that came her way. Like her problems were something she could chew up and swallow down.

"You remember that weird librarian, the *gringo*? He told me that if you eat enough chocolate, chemically, it produces the same feeling as love. If you ask me, Viviana could have eaten every chocolate bar in the county and not have filled the hole that bastard put in her."

X.

Case #: 1798-191.3
Transcript: Dolores Guarecuco
Interviewing Officer: Sheriff Claudio Reynoso &
Dr. Geronimo Diaz
Interview #: 9

"She doesn't have anything to do with this. My mother's been dead fifteen years. There's no reason to talk about her."

[Ms. Guarecuco remained silent for a moment.]

"I won't talk about her."

XI.

Case #: 1798-191.3
Transcript: Deputy Sheriff Jay Sutton
Interviewing Officer: Sheriff Claudio Reynoso
Interview #: 3

"You came to the right man, boss. I didn't work the Guarecuco arson or anything, but my old man did. Haunted him 'til the day he went loony a few years back. Hell, I remember the night it happened. I was just a kid, but you don't forget something like that.

"He came home with an awful stink, I mean terrible. Only time I ever came close to that smell was when we pulled a dead skunk out from under the house. You remember that, don't you? Me and the family went down to Padre Island for the weekend. Imagine that stink, a dead skunk cooking under a house for three days.

"My old man smelt worse than that.

"It was like grease, old, dirty grease. I mean, imagine the worst wind you've ever passed, burp on it, and set that shit on fire. Whatever's left, that was the old man's stink. Lord as my witness, I smelled him three minutes before he even pulled into the driveway.

"Oh, yeah, sorry boss. Well, apparently—and this wasn't in the paper—it was the same old story over there. Guarecuco showed up drunk as usual, finds the wife, and well, beats her something fierce. I mean, you remember that neighborhood. Least three other families down that way. Well, before the fire anyway. Hell, that row cleared the whole street. That smoke, good God, that smoke.

"Guarecuco apparently took that wife of his, dragged her outside. Dolores was in the house and everything. But, he took that woman outside and really laid into her. Didn't even find a whole skull in the ashes so my old man told me. Cheek was all busted open. But, he hit her and he hit her and when she stopped moving, he went out to the shed and got some kindling. That dead fuck made himself a campfire out of his wife. And, boss, I know she'll lie about it until she can't talk, but Dolores saw the whole damn thing. This ain't the kind of world where the Lord is kind enough to spare a child that kind of tragedy."

XII.

Case #: 1798-191.3
Transcript: Manolo Andrade
Interviewing Officer: Sheriff Claudio Reynoso
Interview #: 6

"Sorry, Sheriff. I am not from here. I've only heard stories of the fire. The guys tell me it was a little glow in the distance at first. With this flat land, you can see a fire for miles, so they thought nothing of it.

"They said a stink came with it after a while. Like…the smell of rancid fat hitting the coals. They all looked to the fire and then it flashed like a star. Some say the boom knocked them over, but I'm sure they were lying. Others say they heard a pop. I don't know. I'm not from here."

XIII.

Case #: 1798-191.3
Transcript: Edgar Magnon, Arson Specialist (retired)
Interviewing Officer: Sheriff Claudio Reynoso
Interview #: 8

[Mr. Magnon, former arson consultant on case #0138-919.2, the murder/suicide of the Guarecucos, arrived at the San Casimiro Sheriff's Office at 3:14 p.m. to discuss details of case #0138-919.2.]

"Grease fire. That's the one that'll really get you. I won't rattle on with all kinds of numbers and yearly figures. I'll just say that grease fires are that fellow, Darwin, embodied.

"Most folks see fire and think life's like the cartoons. Douse it with some water, that'll do it. Wrong! That burning oil just springs up, catching on what's already lit until you've got liquid flames eating up everything they touch.

"That's what happened to those Guarecucos. Char-patterns on the ground showed an accelerant, sure. But, that was mostly on the wife's clothing, and it wasn't enough to get a boom like that. I don't hold much stock in small town descriptions, no offense. It's just, I don't know, if there isn't much going on in these towns, every little thing seems more important.

"Anyway, some of the locals said it was a thirty foot ball of flame. I don't believe it, but it sure scorched that ash tree they had. Dry as it is around here, it's a wonder the whole town didn't catch.

"No, he poured something on her, but the kicker, what really got the fire going, that was human fat, my friend. Yes sir, sure as I'm sitting here, human fat can do it. Just think of fat as lard or something, butter even. Cold, room temperature, that stuff is solid. Not rock solid, but solid enough to not splish-splash all over the place. When that woman's clothes caught, all that fat started warming up and quick. Converts to oil by the time the first layers of skin are gone. It's all science from there. Scary, scary science and the devil's physics.

"That fire touches all that oil and you've got yourself a two hundred fifty pound Molotov cocktail. That's probably what caught the husband on fire. Didn't help that polyester was 'in' at the time. His primary injuries, according to the M.E., were severe burns to the forearms and face. Pretty consistent with a defensive position. But, it still didn't account for the burn radius.

"As close as we could figure, that daughter of theirs must've seen it happen. Or heard it happen. All that oxygen getting swallowed up makes a hell of a ruckus. Known a man who popped his eardrum using too much diesel to light a grill.

"Whatever got that girl to come out, got her to come out. I don't know how old she was, but that fellow, Darwin, didn't care. The wife, she was a goner, no saving her. The father would've been scarred up, sure, but he would've lived. Well, maybe if the girl didn't throw a bucket of water on him.

"That alone made that burn radius over eight feet. You think about that, eight solid feet of hell burning despite you. Eating you up. Ain't a worse way to go, if you ask me."

XIV.

Case #: 1798-191.3
Transcript: Dolores Guarecuco
Interviewing Officer: Sheriff Claudio Reynoso & Dr. Geronimo Diaz
Interview #: 9

"Yes, I saw it happen…I saw it all from the window. My father hitting my mother again and again, dragging her like a bag of trash. And he…burned her. He burned her and just watched it happen. He just stood there and watched her scream and thrash in the flames.

"I remember he used to carry a flask in his coat. It had the Guarecuco crest on it. He was reaching for it when my mother got her revenge, when she lashed out at him. I was too young to know that I should have let him suffer. He was…my dad…but…

"It was the screaming. Yes, we feared him. I don't know how many nights I hid at the sound of his car coming into the driveway. But, I didn't think he could scream that way. My mother's screams had died, but they stopped bothering me even then. She always screamed. When he came home late or early. A good mood or a bad one. It got to be another sound to me like doves or a dog's howl in the dark.

"Back then, I didn't think my father could scream… he was the scariest thing in my life, what I had nightmares about, but he screamed like a child. The same shake I heard in my mother was the same one that trembled in his scream. Yes, I did throw the water on him. How was I supposed to know that would happen? My mother was too busy crying to teach me anything useful."

XV.

Case #: 1798-191.3
Transcript: Jaime Raz
Interviewing Officer: Sheriff Claudio Reynoso
Interview #: 2

"Well, I went in because she offered me a beer. It was hot as shit and there I was pushing around a cart in the heat like a damn mule. You'd think there'd be more business, but not like when my father did it. You know what killed it? Killed the whole industry. Bet you can't figure it out.

"Damn, first try. Yeah, air conditioning.

"Even a house used to get hot in the summer, and the kiddos all want a cold treat when they played outside. Well, sometimes, the kid in us never goes away, air-conditioning or not. And, with Dolores, I just thought she liked to eat paletas.

"She offered me a beer, and I said why not. What harm could there be? Get out of the heat and chat her up. I figured if I talked enough, she'd get hungry and eat a paleta, want another one, and do a whole day's work with a beer in my hand.

"Jumped me the second I closed the door. You wouldn't think it, but someone that size can take you down *easy*. And she took me down easy. Practically fell on me, squirming around to get on top of me, already sweating from the effort. Spread on me like a walrus. I couldn't even scream. Too much pressure on my chest. I knew if I shouted, I wouldn't be able to get my breath again. And she just laid there, her voice vibrating through her body, telling me to calm down. When my vision spotted up and went black, I thought I'd died."

XVI.

Case #:1798-191.3
Transcript: Deputy Sheriff Nicholas Egan
Interviewing Officer: Sheriff Claudio Reynoso
Interview #: 5

[Deputy Sheriff Egan was hospitalized after direct contact with the basement of the Guarecuco house. As photographs indicate, at least seven bodies were found, all in various stages of decay. Several were fully clothed, despite showing various signs of post-mortem sexual trauma. After Deputy Sheriff Egan's release, he was brought in for direct questioning.]

"Boss, I don't need to tell you how bad that smelt. I mean, the whole house smelled like a roasted pig just sat on the table and rotted. But, seeing the Guarecuco woman, it's not a wonder why the whole place stank. When I took off after her, she must've been twenty yards from me and already on the other side of her fence. I don't need to tell you what a head-start does for a perpetrator. Hell, my first week, a wetback coming over from Tamaulipas had a three second start on me. I chased him for an hour and only got a mouthful of dust for the trouble.
    "Guarecuco, though. She couldn't move if she wanted

to. I think that's why she got so many of them. They didn't figure her a danger enough, but why would you? I met her a few times before. She seemed a little off, but most country folk are if you ask me.

"How?

"Well, it's got to be something about the area, maybe. The fact that the world kind of gets compressed for these people, like there ain't a damn thing worth knowing or doing fifty miles from this very spot. Yeah, I thought she was off, but nothing had me ready for that basement.

"The doctors say it was some flesh-eating virus I picked up there, and it may be. But, without sounding too superstitious, I think it was just the spirit of the place finally getting out at someone. She'd... she'd actually posed them up, Boss. Like they were dolls. Wouldn't be too hard, I suppose, not with them withered up and flattened like they were. Couldn't weigh more than thirty pounds apiece.

"They were just sitting in there, posed up like they were having a conversation all around the chair. The crime scene crew said it was the chair she tied Jaime Raz to. All those others were posed to look at it...like it was some kinky show.

"I don't think it was a flesh-eating virus at all. I think it was the evil in that place. Damn near took my hand, so the doctors told me."

XVII.

Case #:1798-191.3
Transcript: Jaime Raz
Interviewing Officer: Sheriff Claudio Reynoso
Interview #: 2

"Don't make me talk about the basement.

"No, I don't have to. You can't just convict the bitch on what you found in there? You saw the house?

How can't that be enough? Tell me why I need to talk about it.

"So…if I tell you what she did, she can't use any insanity plea or anything? She'll fry?

"Don't tell me maybe! I want to know that bitch'll cook! Give me your word!

"Fine…I'll tell you all about basement.

"When I woke up, my head was swimming. My body ached from her fat ass, but I think she just rolled me to the stairs and kicked me down them. She was tying me up. I don't know where my clothes went…

[Mr. Raz remained silent for a moment.]

"I know I have to keep going. Just…give me a second.

"All I could see was her, jiggling as she tied my feet to the chair legs. There was some rag or something in my mouth, but I wasn't trying to scream. I was too busy swimming and she finished tying me and saw that I was awake. 'I'm so happy you're not hurt,' she told me. She said it like we were lovers. That's what the look in her eye said to me. That we were lovers, but we weren't. Whatever that whore tells you, I never touched her, not until she forced me. Makes me want to puke just thinking about it.

"She kissed where my lips were covered in tape and moaned like a *pinche vaca*! She told me she'd have me, and I started shaking my head, my whole body. No, no, no! She was disappointed, and stood up to leave. She was going to get something to change my mind, she said.

"I don't care if you think I'm not a man, I was crying. Crying as she waddled up those stairs and locked me down there.

"It took a moment for my eyes to adjust, but when they did, *madre de dios*…I wanted to die. I'd known two of them…two of the dead men staring at me. Juan Royas and Pedro Fabiolo. They were dead and dried, flies and maggots moving out of their empty eyes. I screamed so hard I nearly inhaled the rag in my mouth. I started to choke on it when Dolores came in again. I was glad I was going to die. I knew she couldn't hurry down the steps, and she didn't try. She watched me choke and fall and did nothing. Inched to me as best she could and let out the gag.

"'This'll make it easier,' she told me, two cleaned paleta sticks in her hand. She sat me up and tied my dick with the sticks like some tourniquet. Grunting and moaning as she handled me. I wanted nothing more than to die.

"Then, she lifted up her dress…I…I don't want to talk anymore. I'm going to be fucking sick."

XVIII.

Case #:1798-191.3
Transcript: Dr. Geronimo Diaz
Interviewing Officer: Sheriff Claudio Reynoso
Interview #: 10

"I don't know what good my opinion will do, Sheriff, but I'll give it. Dolores Guarecuco was suffering from numerous traumatic events. The death of one's parents, whatever the circumstances are, leave an individual with mounds of residual mental trauma. For one, the sense of abandonment. It was this, I believe, that led to her excessive eating habits. Well, that and the learned behavior of her mother. She dealt with trauma by finding comfort in food. You wouldn't believe it, but that is quite common.

"The human body, for all its complexities, is a simple machine, like a car or a television. Certain things must be done in order to continue existing. For a car, it is fuel and the driver sees the need for it when their car stops running. But, for people, there are three things that need to be met in order to continue a relatively healthy life. Only three.

"The first is sex. It's burned in our DNA. It links us to every living thing on the planet and beyond. Fish, trees, snakes, whatever, all of these things are driven by a want to procreate. When a human does this, a rush of hormones and enzymes flood the brain, giving us that euphoric feeling after an intense orgasm.

"I'm sorry. This isn't making you uncomfortable, is it? Good.

"Other than sex, there is sleep. The body sends another wave of euphoria when it is tired and the conscious mind allows it time to rest. That is why an afternoon nap seems to invigorate a person. But, the final one is food.

"How can we prolong our species if we have no energy? As a reward for eating, our bodies release the same compound of chemicals so that we may be taught, like Pavlov's dog, that to eat is to feel a form of pleasure. This is the basic principle behind food addiction, nymphomania, and a love of sleep.

"Mrs. Guarecuco, as her daughter watched, showed an addiction to that chemical compound by offsetting the negative stimulus around her—the cheating husband, the beatings, the humiliation. She ate her problems away. Though, an eating addiction is usually followed by an unhealthy self-image, leading, sadly, to more eating to cope with the mental stress. A weak mind leads to a weak body, so they say. But, with Dolores, the abandonment she felt after her parents' death led to extreme feelings of loneliness.

"You see, Sheriff, human beings are social animals. We've lived in small communities for millennia. Even before civilization, humans collected around one another. It is where we learn to be human. Yet, if someone is pushed to the fringes of that community, the mind begins to break down. To function abnormally. There is no outlet for feelings of sadness, anger, or love. It is uncommon, but is recorded, that individuals isolated for long periods of time retreat into themselves. They become their own sustained community.

"As with Dolores, she retreated inside herself and created a fantasy due to her lack of social interactions. Through that fantasy, with no one around to correct it, Dolores looked at the simple dealings of a vendor as being some token of love. Any bit of kindness was an act of chivalry, any hesitation on the part of her victims when it came to her sexual advances was seen as merely gentlemanly foreplay.

"Honestly, if we had a chance to see the world through that poor girl's eyes…why, I'd think we'd go mad from the strangeness of it.

"As for the bodies…again, Sheriff, Dolores is not well. The dead, the way she positioned them, all of it shows an unstable mind. They were not corpses to her, you see, but a community. A group of people she could depend on, to whatever degree she'd invented. I'd imagine she spent many nights in that basement, talking to them. Eating beside them. The smell? I suppose it would be hard to eat in that stink, wouldn't it? But, you forget, Sheriff, the mind.

"The mind is more powerful than any force on Earth. A woman, smaller than you or I, lifted a car off her child, an act only the smallest fraction of a fraction of humanity could do normally. But, her mind allowed her to. I've seen a man put himself in a trance and stand on a roaring fire, scorching hair and the like, but when he leapt off the flames, there was not one blister on his skin. The mind, Sheriff, it is truly a wondrous thing.

"Where we saw a room filled with corpses, Dolores saw a parlor with guests who lifted their cups to her as she descended the stairs. A community that cheered her as she molested those men, probably complimenting her and the passion she roused out of her victims. They were all she had, I suspect. Just those corpses and all the bones."

XIX.

Case #:1798-191.3
Transcript: Dolores Guarecuco
Interviewing Officer: Sheriff Claudio Reynoso &
Dr. Geromino Diaz
Interview #: 9

"Yes, I remember them all. They were all kind to me. All gentle. Some of them took some time to love me, but they all did. Each was perfect in his own way. The way he moved beneath me. The way he moved inside me. I know you don't believe me, but they all loved me. Everything they did was for me. Some were shy, only stopping at my door once a month. Others, they came to me daily until I knew they could no longer hide it.

"I liked the shy ones. They made a lot of noise, but once they understood our love, they were gentlemen and did what I asked of them.

"No, no there is nothing wrong with having so many men in love with you as long as they are in agreement. I asked them all, each and every one when I brought another man into our room. If one of them disagreed, I would just kill him there. Lay on him until all the life was gone.

"My men hardly said no. They wanted me to be happy. It was all they lived for."

—ETC.—

Toño

"I don't know," the man said staring out of his mother's dinged-up hatchback, but she said nothing back. He closed his eyes at the sounds of the century-old trees forming a canopy of leaves that passed at an easy thirty-five miles an hour. Old men in Bermuda shorts watered their lawn while keeping a close eye on the green car they'd never seen in their neighborhood before and when they waved, the man forced a smile and raised his hand to them, silently wondering how anyone could navigate the dirt roads that rattled their suspension. His mother asked him if he said something; he rolled his eyes. "I just don't know."

"About what?" she asked as she turned down Viggie Road and sighed in relief when she felt smooth asphalt under the tires.

"About coming here. I... I don't know. It's weird. I never came here as a kid 'cept those few times and now I'm going to rifle through all his stuff."

"The county said we had to or else they would. There's no one else. And I know there's stuff in there that your grandfather would have wanted you to have."

"What? Old newspapers and cookbooks?" he asked, nestling into the seat-turned three hour home. "Don't give me that look. He never came to see me. Ever. Never called, not even for *your* birthdays. I say we should just turn around, stop off at that little *cantina*," he made sure to accent the word as if he were a full-blooded Kentuckian, "and get drunk."

"Manny," she replied, "why are we going to turn back when we're already here?" She eased the car to a stop and unbuckled her seat belt. The house was a short hall with handmade stone additions taking up the majority of the overgrown lawn. "God," she sighed as she took off her sunglasses. "It brings me back, but...well, it just looked so much better when I was here. I mean, it's not like the lawn sprouted up like this overnight. Dad's only been gone a week," she said and got out. Her heels clattered on the stone disc walkway and when Manny squinted, it looked like she shrunk three feet in a messy lawn, but he followed her all the same to stretch his legs. The old screen door was more tatters than barrier and a flattened gecko, dried brown, clung gargoyle-like inside the door jamb. Pale yellow paint flecks cracked like dead twigs off the walls.

The unlit interior smelt of aged paper and dusty ink. He fumbled around for a light switch, but only rattled old wooden frames that hung crooked from hastily hammered roofer's nails. The lights flared on and the ceiling fan whirred to life and the room hissed with movement. "Huh, still remember the old place," Gale said and watched the fan pick up speed, smelling the years engrained in the brown shag carpeting and wallpapered walls of light blue print, and her son pulled on a ceramic cardinal dangling on the end of a beaded chain to stop the spinning machine.

They waited for the piles of paper to settle.

He looked at the crowded walls, determining the peeling wallpaper served as an interesting border to all the black and white pictures. "Kind of avant-garde if you really think about it," Manny scoffed. "We've got to look through all of this stuff?"

"Every single bit of it. Come on," she said over her shoulder as she went down the hall loudly and shouted. "Oh-my-God! He didn't even change my room! Manny, come here and look. Oh! It just brings me back." She had both her hands pressed to her face and her wide eyes were glowing teary dew drop light in the dusty room when he came in. The twin bed sat cramped up against the wall with its foot touching the edge of a desk and old Nancy Drew novels stood in a musty line, their spines thumbed and frayed. All along the walls hung posters with their corners torn off from thumb-tacks still buried into the sea-foam paint. Lining the window sill, mindless stuffed bears and cats that had long lost their childish zeal, sat limp and lifeless. The A/C kicked on and blew cool air from the large grated vent in the corner. Gale ran on the dirty carpet to one animal she called "Mr. Pinochle!" and hugged it until she took in its scent and flung it to the bed. "Oh my Lord! How can a stuffed bunny smell like eggs?"

He sniffed the air with his hands in his pockets and shrugged. "I think it's the best smelling thing in the house."

"I'd agree since you made the room smell so smoky."

"Come off it, ma. They used to catch you puffing away in high school."

"Those were different times," she said shooting a glare at him; he didn't look convinced. "We didn't know about cancer and stuff back then. Everybody did it."

"Hate to tell you, surgeon general, but everybody smokes now."

She said nothing to him as though he'd been silent and went out of the house. Her keys fell when she tried to jab them into the trunk's keyhole, but she held her cursing tongue and called out to him loudly, with the elongated inflections of a woman yelling at her seven year old college graduate. He helped her lug her matching black luggage into the house which fought them with each step, gripping their bags with tight halls and narrow doorways. Holding her floral tote bag, she told him to watch the doors when he passed them; rolling his eyes, he coughed whenever the luggage cracked against the wooden jambs and she blamed it on the smoking.

He dropped the luggage in her old room, but her call prompted him to lug them further into the house: she would be sleeping in the main bedroom with its soft, broken-in mattress, and he'd enjoy the rank smell of a sealed vault opened after twenty years. "I'm going to take a nap," she said before the rusted creak of bed springs groaned loud through the thin walls and he dropped her bags, taking his single duffle bag over his shoulder to her room. He opened it, shoved his arm down to his shoes at the bottom of it, stuck his fingers into the sneakers, and quietly took out the few grams of schwag.

It was fluffy and seedy, breaking easily on an old math quiz with a bright red C+ on its corner that he found in a drawer. He tossed the stems and seeds into the thin plastic sandwich bag. The Tops rolling papers were running low and he wondered if he'd have to buy a pouch of Buglers since he doubted a small town would have any selection in rolling papers. The joint was short but robust and fit easily into his pocket. He carefully stepped towards the entrance to the backyard, passing an old Mayan calendar sticking its tongue out towards the shuttered window across from it.

The backyard roared to life as he opened the door. Birds of all kinds, cardinals and sparrows and green jays and hummingbirds, tore through the checkerboard of droppings on the yard's ground and into the sky. "Sweet shit," Manny gasped. The yard was crowded by two massive tree trunks that had little plastic bird feeders screwed into the old wood and between the two living columns stood a granite bird bath with two fat children stooped down as if looking at their reflection in the murky green water. He found the least stained chair and parked it with its back to the tall wooden fence.

His joint was fresh and harsh, forcing him to cough into a rag he'd brought from home until it felt as though his heaves expanded the very reality around him more and more, to the point of breaking and his final, throat clearing cough was the needle to reality's balloon and the burst sounded clearly like the sway of leaves and passing of old pick-up trucks.

With relaxed eyes, he slowly examined everything within an arm's length with the interest of an entomologist, horticulturalist, and artist rolled into a single glance. Between the nearest tree and fence, a yellow spotted orb weaver feasted on a June bug with tiny tears in the center of its thin web that shimmered like an iridescent maze in the wind. Above him, spotted auburn butterflies shoved their black and yellow faces into flowers like thin legged dogs, opening and closing their folded wings as they gripped their cups with more fervor and they were dried. He laughed, took a long drag, and looked at the chipping wall in front of him and the large prison-like vent with crisscrossed wire. The smoke tickled his throat and twin glints of jungle green flashed in the darkness, turning a surprised gasp into a series of coughs that only half-found themselves in his rag. He looked again as the smoke and phlegm cleared, but all he saw was the orange of the sun dully reflected on the wires and the shadows they held prisoner.

"Tasty," he chided as he soon forgot what prompted the burning in his lungs.

Manny felt the dust forming a thin layer on his skin though he tried to brush it off his pant legs. He flipped through old photos, brown with age, and boxes of Polaroid's. There were dozens of his mother as a quirky preteen on the ranches surrounding the town and all that changed between them was pose and dress, but the same dense landscape in all.

"Oh, that was my grandfather's ranch. What," Gale asked the corner of the room, "what was its name?" She tapped her chin repeatedly and he sat there waiting. "I can't remember, but," she said, jumping back into the original tempo. "Anyway, we used to go out there all the time: riding horses, shooting, cooking. Oh, we practically lived there in the summers. And, did you know, the land had been in my mom's family for eighty five years before that? If we had gotten it, that land would have been ours over a hundred years. That's some real history."

"It'd be kind of pointless though," Manny said finally. "It's too far out of the way and I know I couldn't live here."

"What? How could you say that? This place would be charming to live a quiet life."

"Too quiet for me."

"Oh," she said and it seemed her words straightened her posture.

"Don't give me that look," Manny said as he looked back at the photos piled in front of him. He only glanced at them and threw them randomly into the piles Gale had demanded they use to organize them. "All I'm saying is that there aren't but a thousand people, so said that marker, and I ask where they are because there certainly isn't two hundred houses in this town--"

"Yes there is!"

"Not the point," he said. "Too little to do. There is one bar and a dancehall, that, if I saw correctly, is also the bingo parlor on Tuesdays and Thursdays. So, sorry, I need a little more to do. I swear it would push me to drugs. Or just a boozer--"

"You know that runs in our genes."

"I'm very aware."

They said nothing for a long time before he found a photo worth looking at twice. It looked to be his mother standing in front of a restaurant with her father's brown suited arm draped over her shoulder and there was an odd looking creature, strangely ape-like, on his arm attached by a leash. Something struck him as worth questioning and he handed the photo over to Gale.

Her squeal of delight nearly deafened him and she looked at it for a moment, then at him, then back at the photo again. "This was my father's first business. He had it going before I was born. Oh, I was just a little girl and oh, my face is just *precious*. Oh, but that thing always made me feel a bit uncomfortable." She stopped and looked it over, inch by inch.

"That's what I was asking about."

"What? Oh, well. That was Toño. He was the restaurant's little mascot. The old sign had that Chilean Whooping Monkey--that's what that is--on it. Dad did that since back then, not a lot of the workers could read English, but everybody knew who Toño was. Oh, it was so funny," she laughed. "He used to wear a little uniform and a little sombrero and dad would sell little ramekins of seed so the customers could feed him and oh, once he got into the beer and oh, that poor little thing was burping and stumbling and I remember my father carrying him and he was so long that it looked like a monkey faced dishtowel."

"What happened to the little guy?"

"Oh, well, it was the strangest thing, so I heard. My parents always worked the restaurant alone, but when I was getting older, they needed to have another set of hands and--Oh, what was his name--David! Yes, David. Anyway, David was a strange man, real flirty. God! He even flirted with me once and I was only thirteen. But, one night, he was doing the same with my mother--oh, she was so pretty then. I'm sure he winked at her, gave her a 'che-che' when she was going to the back and well, my dad went to go tell him something about it. They argued real low so no one else could hear it, but when David put his ear close, little Toño--how drunk that monkey *was*--jumped right off my dad's shoulder. You wouldn't think it, but those tiny teeth," she said to the air and Manny looked down at the picture in his hands and at the four fang-like canines poking out of its open maw. "Well, they just tore up that poor man's throat. Cleared out the whole restaurant with his half-drunk howls and leaping all round that place, getting flung around by his little leash with a tiny bell on it. They used to tell me they heard all that hooting and howling and jingling for a clear mile, but I never heard it. They didn't even come home that night. Oh, I'll never forget it, I was late to school in the morning and I wore--"

"What happened to the *monkey*?"

"I don't know," Gale replied, shaking her head. "They must have set him loose which probably killed the poor little thing."

"It killed somebody."

"It didn't *kill* David. But, oh, he made him pretty much deformed. He couldn't talk above a whisper and his neck was so marred up that he looked like a burn victim. Serves him right for getting too close to a wild animal and a drunk one at that." They heard the grainy clatter of something moving in the vents above them, tearing their attention away from the photos. "It's a wonder that there's not more rats in this nest."

"I'm sure all the vents help."

"I swear, my father could run a business, but he built this house like he wanted to shelter every field mouse in the county."

They followed the sounds with their eyes, watching the vent as though the sound was visible as it bounded deeper into the old house and his mother shivered at the thought of being covered in coarse, black shavings of rodent hair. "I hate rats," she said. "Did you still want to stay somewhere else?" she asked as if ready to leave the place, but he only shrugged.

"Eh, I've slept in worse places than this."

"Like?" she exclaimed.

"Don't ask what you don't want to know."

The men crawled out of the *monte* in droves as the setting sun chased them into the lit town and all the old pick-ups rattled down the dirt roads and pot hole ridden pavement towards Rosario's and its back lit plastic flamenco dancer with a rose between her teeth and a tray of tequila shots above her head. Manny made a place for himself at the corner nearest to the open wooden doors and the old barkeep, bent with a full beard of salt-and-pepper hair, kept a trained eye on him, but made him wait a full five minutes in a bar filled by twenty people to serve him. "Give me the strongest and the cheapest tequila in here," he said to the man. "Looking to get plowed fast."

"Made from our own agave," the bartender told him as he poured the pungent brown-amber liquor into the shot glass. It hadn't touched the bar in front of him before Manny snatched it up and gulped it. His face tightened by the stuff hissing acrid smoke into his throat, Manny tapped the bar for another and the bartender obliged. He repeated this three times and as he tapped for the fifth, the bartender popped open a can of cola and placed it there. "N-no, no," Manny slurred. "This," he tapped the lacquered bar, "means another shot."

"I don't care what it means to you. Take it easy, I don't want you killing someone on the road."

"Ain't driving. I walked here."

"Pretty long walk considering I've never seen you before. This your first time in town?"

"In about twenty years and I don't even remember what this place was like."

"Hasn't changed much," the bartender said.

"No surprise there," Manny replied and drank his soda.

"You got a name?"

"I'll tell you what," Manny said with a mischievous look, "I know how these towns work. You guys are starved for anything to keep you entertained. So, if you've got a shot to give, I've got a name to match it." The old man considered it, then poured a shot for him, which he took greedily and rapped it on the bar between them. "Real tasty stuff you got here and the name's Manuel Alvarez."

"Alvarez? As in Gustavo Alvarez?"

"It'll cost you," Manny laughed. The bartender paid. "Yes, sir. Gustavo was my grandfather. I'm Gale's kid."

"Oh," the bartender sighed with his eyes on the floor. "We were all sorry about Gus; he was a hell of a guy."

"Only met him a handful of times."

"Well, you can trust me on it. He was a big name around here. With that restaurant of his--"

"Toño's?

"That's the one! Best *gorditas* for twenty miles."

"Hey, you wouldn't know where that monkey he had went off to?"

"Nope. Figured it would be dead by now. A monkey can't live for more than ten years, I don't think. And it wouldn't get far around here. It's harsh land out there and a bobcat could get to it as easy as a rattler or a *javelina*. No, that little thing died a long time ago."

Manny considered his words and settled on pulling a few bills out of his pocket, but the bartender stuck his hand out to stop him. "Call them on the house. Like I said, we're real sorry about Gus."

"It isn't for the shots, it's for the rest of the bottle." The bartender lifted the bottle from behind the bar and held it out for him.

"Give my best to your mother," he said as Manny, lips wrapped around the bottle's neck, walked into the morbidly quiet streets.

All the houses were in neat rows with dirt alleys connecting neighbors with communal lanes and the tequila was nearly gone but Manny fought the urge to go back to Rosario's and kept his journey as straight as his wobbling feet could. The homes were all short stacks of brickwork bordered with flowers and blooming cacti with tiny ornaments hanging in the dark windows from suction-cups. Once in a while, a pair of eyes would meet his through an open window and he'd raise his bottle to them. He found it amusing how quickly they shut their windows. Turning onto Viggie and spotting his mother's car, he drained the last of his bottle then flipped it in his fingers to toss it like a pipe-bomb onto the empty street. He watched it whoop through the air and he threw up a victorious fist when it smashed into a thousand stars reflecting the street lamps. Curtained lights from four houses around flipped on and he fell onto the ground hard as he tried to skitter away, but was well into the shadows of a house's elm before men and shotguns made their hasty appearance. The shouts of gruff voices demanding "Who's there!" made his slip into his grandfather's house an odd relief, but he quickly blamed it on the tequila.

He dreamt the same as he slept: drunkenly.

His bleary eyes opened into darkness and on his bare chest, he felt a strong rush of mechanical wind lapping up his sweat like a whisper that grew louder and louder until he felt as though he was gripping onto the vent's grate like an anchor to save him from being blown away and for a moment, he stood in the blackness, gazing groggily into the steel tubing, as if waiting for something awful to appear. Four fangs, white as chalk, emerged first and the jaws were filled with tiny, flat teeth dripping froth onto the vent's bottom, advancing slowly until its eyes were twin flames of green lasering towards him with blind hate, knocking him onto his back, which struck something soft and musty. He backed away from it as the creature moved through the vent like some specter, gliding slowly through the space between them with its eyes straight ahead, though as it hung in the air, it shot both its eyes at him. Following the small rounded head, with sideburns of matted fur dangling down past its sharp jaw, no longer black but grey, its body moved towards him, letting its long hairy arms drag on the implied ground. With its hands turned up and glowing, a bright red scar shown on the side of its left hand, extending from knuckle to wrist. All on it were rags which it wore same as the wrinkled expression on its tired, yet terrible face. He felt its spindly arms grab his shirt and scale him until the creature stood with both feet planted on his chest. It took hold of Manny's mess of hair and with a strength that was odd for its size, it pulled their faces closer together until they could both distinctly smell each other. After its long inhalation, it roared into Manny's face and the force that sent spittle flying and the creature's cheeks slapping blew his hair back and he tried to cover his face from the noxious assault that seemed like a cold blade against his throat, but the terrible sound inside his head pulled Manny from the false reality between his ears and jerked him out of bed, onto the floor, and back into a fitful sleep.

He awoke with a hangover and was lying on the ground. He shook the sleep out of him and sat up on the bed, wondering how he'd turned up on the floor. Laughing, he thought back to the previous night, and the glint of steel beside him caught his eye. He reached out, plucking the bare razorblade off Gale's old nightstand and rubbed his face with his clammy hand. "Huh," he said, "tried to do plenty drunk; never tried shaving, though." He scratched his bare chin, shrugged, and tossed the piece of steel back onto the desk.

He never knew the weight of paper. Yet, as he pulled the double-bagged load of it into the backyard, he found respect for it in the quickly growing knots in his lower back. Gale had told him to burn all of them, the ones too blurry to fit in one of her deeply organized and labeled scrapbooks and all of the grainy effigies of people she never met in places she'd never been. He pulled the cleanest seat as close to the red-clay chimenea and took out crumpled handfuls to feed into it. He doused the old pictures with an old can of lighter fluid, lit a match, and tossed it inside; the boom of too much fluid nearly sent him to the ground, but he pulled a tightly rolled joint out of his pocket and sighed a silent thanks to fire itself for producing the pungent, masking smoke. He took a single picture of his grandfather sitting atop a faded green tractor surrounded by jeering brown faces and let its corner catch on fire to light his smoke.

He watched the old glossy faces curl into themselves like frightened insects and grow thinner and thinner until they were only twisted husks of ash that he piled more pictures onto and in his growing bleariness, he thought he was staring into hell. He took the final drag off his joint and tossed the roach into the flames, which ate it quickly. He wasn't through half of the bag before he had to stop.

"Manny!" Gale cried from inside the house. "Manny! Come here!"

He groaned and pulled himself up by his knees. Moving into the house, he followed her calls to the furthest end of the house. "What's going on?" he asked when he saw her teetering on an old stool and her fingers wrapped around the silver trim of the air vent.

"God, you smell like smoke," she muttered, then continued her soft pulls. She said nothing though he stood in the doorway. "I wish you wouldn't smoke."

"It's those burning pictures--"

"Did you just leave them burning out there! The whole house could go up!"

"Well, I just dumped them all in, doused them real good--used the whole can--and came in here."

"Are you serious!"

"No."

"Oh." She pulled on the grate, but it only gave a bit before snapping back onto the wall.

"What did you need?" he asked, but got no response until he turned to leave.

"I need your help with this. It's so dusty in here. I want to clean the inside of this," she said and pulled at it harder, but Manny touched her shoulder to stop her. Being near a foot taller, he looked at the stuck metal, reached out and flipped the two securing latches, which forced the grate to hang awkwardly on the square opening and with a metallic click. The sound of tiny feet moving away from them had her hopping off the stool. "I hate, hate, *hate*, rats!"

"Do you need anything else?" he asked. In response, she handed him a rag which she motioned to the vent with. He rolled his eyes and went to it. Pulling his shirt up above his nose, he dipped his arm into it and collected the years of dust in small circular motions. The flat scratch of paper made him toss his rag into the vent and he pinched the wrinkled corner of something and brought it up to his face. "Damn, did he just shove photos everywhere?" He puffed his piney-smelling breath, bursting the scratchy cloud of dirt off of the torn picture. It was an age darkened picture of the whole family: his mother was smiling in her pigtails wrapped in her father's arm which finished in a wicked scar from wrist to knuckle, her mother stood on the opposite side of his wide shoulders with a warm grin, and Toño sat howling on his paternal back. Yet, the face of his grandfather had been eaten away with tiny nibbles, making the picture look like the tiny monkey had a body too large for its head.

"What happened to grandpa's hand?" he asked.

"Oh? I don't know. He always had that scar. He told us he got it from a Mexican dog fight, but he also said he got it from filleting a fish he caught when he was in his teens--said it was six feet long and had a set of human teeth--but he was always telling stories."

"Took a lot of pictures for a storyteller," Manny said flatly.

He paid his money and Rosario's bartender placed a plastic jug of foul smelling tequila in front of him. "Nice bottle," Manny breathed along with smoke from his slowly burning cigarette.

"It's to keep you from breaking it."

"Why would I break it? Can't drink from something busted."

"I agree, but it didn't stop you from breaking the last one."

"Wasn't me," he replied in the rasp of a man holding a great lungful of smoke at bay with sheer willpower.

The bartender smiled and leaned forward. "Kid, this is a small town and *you know* how small towns work: people talk. When the Leindo's disowned their son for wanting to go to clown college, the whole town knew before he finished packing and when the Stillmeadow kid got pinched for smoking dope, well, I knew about it before the paper came out the very next morning."

"This town has a paper?"

"Yes, sir."

"How many pages?"

"A whole fifteen with local and national and sports and some comics for the kids."

"You don't say," Manny muttered to his filter.

"So, with a town like this, you don't think everyone knew Gus Alvarez's grandson was stumbling around last night half crazy on the Rosario Special?"

"Guess you don't have much in the way of privacy around here."

"Heh, you want privacy, go back to the big city. Here, you got to give up some things for the quiet life. Yeah, when my wife found a *sancho* two towns over, everyone knew, but they were all looking out for me, making sure I don't look like a fool. They don't do that if you've got privacy."

Manny stubbed out his cigarette after lighting another with it. The bartender left to attend an old, dusty couple with stained teeth and smudged fingers. He drank in smoky silence before the conversation caught up again. "You said you knew my grandfather real well?"

"Sure did. Played football together in high school."

"You know how he got that scar on his hand?"

He thought about it as he wiped down brandy glasses and placed them behind the bar in neat rows. "He told me he got it falling out of a tree before I moved here. Why?"

"Just wondering," Manny chortled then finished the rest of his glass and took his plastic jug for another walk, nearly getting clipped in the face by the bar door opening. He stopped in front of her and optically drank her like the drunk he was. She was short compared to him, but he was glad for it since it afforded him a chance to stare down her low-cut shirt at her pair of round, caramel colored breasts. She wore too much make-up, darkening her small yet juicy lips and her almond eyes slowly went from his chest to his face.

"You're not from around here, are you?" she asked through a smile.

"No. I'm not," he said. "Bartender," he shouted over his shoulder without taking his eyes off of the brown haired girl, "get me another glass. Me and this little lady are going to do some drinking." He moved his face closer to hers, "Unless," he said barely above a whisper, "you'd rather drink alone." She considered it a moment, then took his arm into hers and led him to a corner table. He looked at her as if she were going to disappear and she coyly fluttered her eyelashes at him. He filled her glass while he drank straight from the jug. "So, what's the story behind a small town gal like yourself?"

She laughed into her painted hand and rested her head on her arm. "You know, that is what I love about visitors. I know so much about them and they don't know a bit about me. I'm--"

"Christine!" the bartender barked before leaning onto the counter-top. Both sets of eyes went across the room. "Your daddy know you're in here?"

"My daddy doesn't know a lot of things! Now leave me be. I ain't doing nothing wrong. Just talking to this nice fellow."

"We all know what your talk leads to," he shot back.

"Shut your mouth and leave me alone!" she shouted then turned back un-phased to Manny who sat giggling and wide-eyed. "What's so funny, Mr. *Alvarez*?"

"Small town people. But don't worry *Christine*," he edged closer to her. "We're all a little dirty, you know? And, plus, I'll tell you right now, I'm a sure thing. And, if I'm a sure thing, and you're a sure thing, then why don't we just enjoy it?"

She laughed. "Why don't we just go back to your place?"

"Oh, it'll ruin it. I want to really want it. I want to watch you and sneak little peaks down your shirt and watch you walk to the bathroom and just wonder what kind of panties you've got on until the animal in my blood is on fire and I just can't stand it."

"That sounds fine," she said leaning forward a bit.

"So," he said as he lit a cigarette, "you say you know something about me. What can you possibly know other than my name, maybe not even th--"

"Manuel Alvarez. You're here with your mother, Gale. You've been here two days and you walked home drunk as can be last night. Broke a bottle three blocks from here. Oh, you smoke Parliaments too," she said in spitfire succession, then perked her shoulders and giggled; he let the ash accumulate on his cigarette.

"Well, that is certainly something. You don't have much to do around here, do you?"

"Oh, I keep myself entertained."

"I'm *sure* you do. But, we're not going to talk about that. No use talking about a fact." They drank and he refilled her cup and they polished off the bottle. "So, did you know my grandfather?"

"Yes," she giggled through her smile. "I liked him a lot. He was real nice to me and, well, I was real nice to him."

"If you mean what you sounded like, that's gross. And if you don't," he came close to her again, "I like the way you talk."

"Thank you, but that's not what I meant. All the little girls had a crush on him, but no one got worried. He was so good looking. You really don't look like him," she laughed.

"Oh, aren't you precious."

"You're cute but you don't look like him. And, you know, they used to say he was impotent since he was a young guy. So, it was like he was begging for little kids to like him. At the festival, they would bust his balls about it, but he'd always say right back, 'My one shot's living in the city with her son,' and would wink. He was a really nice man. I remember--"

"You know," he interrupted. "I can't wait as long as I thought," he said quickly with his eyes on her pert breasts. He snatched her hand and his plastic jug, giving the bartender a wink that looked nothing like old Alvarez's and they were four steps into the darkness, spotted with tiny streetlamp islands of light, before Rosario's door swung closed behind them.

She felt young. Her skin tight and slick about the parts gravity waited lecherously for, which filled his hands supply. The bed was cramped with sheets that reeked of age, but when he pulled her on top of him, the space mattered little. Tucking her wavy brown hair behind her ear, she straddled him in her tight jeans, rubbing the space between her thighs against him, and eased out of her shirt, letting her breasts bounce in their push-up cups, before leaning back into his arms. She kissed him hard, pulling at his lip caught between her teeth, and whispered, "Won't your old lady wake up?" She slept with veins filled with prescribed promises and he, snapping his fingers against the bra's clasp, which gave easy, told her so. Kissing him, she looked up at the bed posts, sighing a coy giggle into his mouth. "Want to try something fun?" she winked and when she dangled her bra in front of him, he smiled the smile of understanding.

They switched positions and as she manhandled his clasped jeans with one hand; he wrapped her hand in her black underwear, then grabbed the other and tangled it around her wrist. He quickly looped the straps through the intertwined posts and clasped it. Leaning back to admire the young thing, legs rubbing together, and her round breasts, nipples erect from a mix of cold air leaking from the vent and anticipation, heaved up and down as she licked and bit on her lip. Though tight, her jeans slipped off her legs easily and he whipped them off her pink toes before they were fully clear.

Her hand strained against the posts and she squealed in delight; he didn't bother to push his pants down past his knees. The feel of her skin against him sent his mind reeling and he fought a quick mental battle between finishing in her before he ejaculated loudly between her ass cheeks.

He kissed her hard, snapping the bra's clasps open, and moved off the bed, watching her still writhing fingers searching spider-like in that beautiful triangle, getting her fingers slick as she watched him dress. Manny pulled his pants up, buckled his jeans, and tapped her foot, announcing, "I'll be right back for round two," and she bit down on her wet index finger. He watched her for a moment and snorted a small laugh before walking out into the hall. His weight shifting the shag carpet made the stacked papers crinkle like dead leaves in the wind.

The bathroom smelt sterile, though it was doubtful it was cleaned since the day they'd purchased the design, which Manny deemed somewhere in the mid-sixties, and the blue bathmat left granular passengers on the bottoms of his bare feet. He lifted the plastic toilet lid and a sharp hiss burst out from the bowl. For an instant, the flat serpentine head of a coiled diamond back, eyes narrow and tongue cutting into water that bubbled from the speed of its tail vibrating, stared up at him. He slammed the toilet seat down and it bucked up as if hit by a tiny battering ram and he roared, "Sweet shit!" at the top of his lungs. The snake pushed its head out of the bowl. Its four foot length easily forcing the light plastic open and spotted Manny in short order. It curled around the base of the toilet, then coiled for a strike.

Manny lifted the blue bathmat and held it before him like a matador. He screamed when it struck, its fangs punching through the old rug, and behind him Christine, underwear half on with one arm covering her breasts, said, "What's all the noise about--" and she spotted the snake and screamed. It struck again to a drum line of Manny's shit-shit-shits.

"Would you shut up!" Manny bellowed at the snake though it was aimed at the still screaming girl behind him.

"What's going--" Gale said as she came into the room. "Oh my God! What is that!" She took a step to the wall, bumping Christine's bare shoulders. "Who the hell is this?" she demanded. "Manuel! What's going--"

"Would the both of you shut the fuck up!" Manny spat.

The rattlesnake hissed at them and shot out of its spring-like coil, catching the rug again. It shook its head against the cloth, its hooked fangs caught inside its fibers. Manny dropped the rug, stomping on the spot he assumed the snake's head to be, but struck the solid floor instead. The snake shook violently beneath the rug and Manny, amidst the shrill screams of his audience, took the lid off the commode and lifted it over his head. He struck the top of its head, spraying their female ankles with sharp grains of bone and meat, and the porcelain broke into two halves, which he slammed down again breaking the pieces in half, and so on, until he stood their lobbing ceramic pebbles at the death shroud so fresh the inhabitant still went through its death throes. Yet, the duet trying their hardest to release their apprehensive fear through their open mouths still continued their song.

"The both of you!" he yelled at them. "Shut it already! God damn," he muttered and lifted the rug off the battered reptilian sausage and he breathed a sigh of relief at the sight of it. "How the hell did this get in here? Piece of shit town."

"Didn't you hear it?"

He didn't respond at first, but reached out and picked up its coiled tail. "I'm sure I would've if it still had a rattle," he said as he examined the bleeding stump of a tail that showed like a pink ring of muscle round a bone core; from the scratches around the length that wasn't bruised, it looked as though something had bitten down on its tail and torn off the signature of its species.

"You're a damn regular now aren't you?"

"Nothing else to do around here," Manny replied as he watched his shot glass fill soundlessly. "Hey, do you know what eats rattlesnakes?"

"Besides people?" he asked and thought about it a moment, clearing both his thoughts and the murk of the glass mug with the same motion. "Well, a whole bunch of things. For one, you got hawks and falcons and the like. They'll eat them. You've also got your roadrunners, they'll kill 'em. Hell, even other snakes eat them. Black indigos and king snakes eat them all the time. Why do you ask?"

Manny's eyes went to the opening door down the bar as Christine walked in with a simple country girl, blonde and cross-eyed, and said, "I'm just wondering. Found a snake in the house with its rattle missing. Just trying to figure out what did it."

"So, eh," the bartender said leaning forward as they both watched Christine's tight jeans and she kept her eyes trained away from them, going so far as to wave at an imaginary person her cross-eyed friend couldn't find, though she desperately tried, to dodge having to greet him. "How'd it go with little Christine last night?" he asked with a wink.

Manny smiled before he drank and told the old man to watch him carefully if he wanted to learn something. "Hey Christine! When are we going for round two?" he yelled in the near empty place.

"Fuck you!" she shot back, then sat with her back to him.

"Well," the bartender laughed. "At least you had round one." He refilled Manny's shot glass.

"Hell of a round it was," Manny sighed as he tilted his head back, greedily accepting the harsh brew.

"Yeah, most of us say the same."

Manny nearly spit the tequila in his throat out at the word 'us.' "What do you mean? You've hit that also?" The old man tried to deny it, but just laughed. "Oh," Manny sputtered as he wiped his mouth with his cupped hand. "Man, I knew she wasn't an amateur, but just how many people in this town has she fucked?"

"Kid, you're about as intimate with this town as you're going to get after lying with that one. You can go to any street, stop on any block, close your eyes, spin around till you fall, and where you're looking after that is more likely than not a house little Christine left her little panties in. But, that's just this town. You're a regular citizen of the county now. Haha!"

"That's fucking gross old man," he gagged. He threw a twenty onto the counter and pointed to the bottle he'd been drinking from. The old man, laughing behind his hand, passed it to him. Manny stood and left without turning and drank as he walked, but the bartender called out to him.

"Did she tell you to tie her up with her bra too?" he laughed

"Shut the fuck up, old man!" both Manny and Christine bellowed.

Manny tried to swig down the remainder of the jug, but his body couldn't take any more and he took it from his lips to examine how much was left: a finger's worth of liquor rippled at the bottom. He lazily took another drag of his joint, held it, and blew a lungful into the night air. With another small hit, he decided to toss the rest in the jug with a hiss of smoke and tossed it over the fence behind him. Supporting his sitting position with his elbows, Manny stared at the blank wall in front of him and mused that it was staring back at him, that something was staring back at him. He focused his eyes until he thought he could see the granular pits of the old bricks and nearly reached out to them, but an empty rumble in his gut pulled him to his feet.

"Wonder what there is to eat around here?" he asked the air and went inside.

In the kitchen, he turned on the electric stovetop and looked for a skillet to use. He found it beside the cleaning products beneath the sink and wondered how his grandfather had ever been a chef. A greasy sponge swiping dryly over the surface was enough for him. He placed the skillet on top of the burner and opened the fridge. All of the items he needed were in clear plastic cases: tortillas, bacon, eggs, and individually wrapped cheese slices. He heated the tortilla until crisp tumors bubbled on both sides, then he threw them onto the counter with nothing under them. He threw the eggs onto the hot skillet and watched the scrambled mess go from clear mix tinged with yellow to a fluffy white.

He heard something land softly across the kitchen, but decided he'd only imagined it. The Rosario Special loved to play tricks. He continued to cook until the sound of a bare blade scraping out of its wooden block base shot his eyes open and forced him to take hold of the skillets warm handle tightly. "You want some of this, ma?" he asked without turning around and waited, but no answer came. He looked over his shoulder, yet the oddity that filled his vision, though it could stand upright on the counter easily, pulled him around as good as any rough arm.

The creature stood only a few feet tall, but he could see the sinew working under its fur, which started from the top of its head and went down to its feet. Its face was apish with long strands of graying hair, tangled with the bones of rat digits, and it wore a necklace strung together from old hair with a brown stained snake rattle resting in the center of its chest. It brought a small filet knife up in front of it, casting a shadow over its green, human eyes that hid in a veil of hair. The side-burns, grown strangely like cartoon-ish paintbrushes, came down past its jaw which closed at a bizarre angle as it tried to snap its four massive canines at him.

Both stood still, not daring to breathe, until Manny uttered the single word, "Toño." The creature howled into a mad leap with the knife held above its rage warped face with both its tiny stained hands. Toño met the hot skillet, trailed by scattering eggs, and yelped as the heated metal singed its fur and sent it roughly against the wall. It wasted no time, getting to its feet and tearing towards the corner of the room. It climbed up the cabinets as if they had footholds and it poised itself for another assault, but it lowered its blade when Gale came charging in the room with her hand covering her eyes. "God damn it, Manny! Who's here now?"

Manny couldn't look at her, only at the tiny tribal creature standing wild-eyed opposite him. "Open your eyes, mom," he said in whisper.

"Why would I--"

"*Mi hija,*" the creature spoke in a grumbling tone like loose funeral dirt cascading into a hole. Gale opened her eyes and Toño reached out to her slowly with his scarred left hand. "*Mi sangre,*" it muttered and forced a crooked grin. She took in the full image of it, nappy hair handing in tresses and knife lowered at its side like a purposeless spear.

"Toño?" she gasped; its canines gleamed in the light as it smiled wider.

"*Si, mija. Es tu padre.*"

"What?" she spat. "Gustavo was my--"

"*Gustavo,*" it said, lowering its eyes. "*Era mi cuate. El siempre fué tu padre. Nada más, mija. Ven p'acá,*" it grumbled, but its voice had done nothing to the woman save sending a liquefying jolt through her, bringing her down to her knees beside the countertop. Her hand slowly rose past her throat to cover her quivering lips. It took a step forward chanting, "*Mija, mija.*" She vomited; the gastric juices spilled between her fingers and onto her green pajamas. "*Esta enfermo, mija?*" it asked and it took all of her not to convulse into a dry heave.

"Disgusting," she whimpered. Then the paleness of her face gave into red as the blood rushed back into her cheeks. "He isn't cold in the ground, you disgusting animal!" she shouted with tears rimming in her eyes.

Toño stopped his advance as if he'd been slapped and the shaking that ran through it rattled the bones tangled in its dusty fur. "*Repugnante?*" it asked slowly. Its chest heaved in great gasps and its tiny fingers wrapped the knife tightly before it shot the quivering woman a glare. "*Bueno... soy un animal repugnante!*" it howled with all its canines showing a dingy yellow in the kitchen's fluorescent light. In an instant, it moved to the edge of the counter like a tiny cliff diver and jumped like a bullet towards her. Manny swung the skillet to catch it, but Toño, contorting like a falling cat, passed harmlessly over it, landing at her knees. It plunged the blade deep into her thigh and tore the knife free. Gale planted a foot in its exposed chest, knocking it back into the cabinets.

The bones rattled rapidly as it shook the stars out of its eyes. Manny swung the skillet down like a hatchet, resounding gong like on the floor which sent a disrupting vibration through the metal cookware up to his shoulder. Toño roared and scrambled up his arm on all fours, spinning around his head wildly until it stopped in front of his face. Its small, needle-like claws buried into Manny's right eye, popping the optical membrane, which oozed its milky white contents through the quickly shutting eyelid.

In a spastic, turning fit, Manny flung the wild animal away from him, to bounce on the hot stove, which caught its oily hair on fire. Toño squealed as it ran from them, passing a roll of paper towels and the fire licked lecherously at it and a pile of rags, soaked with cleaner, that burst into flames. The smoldering creature hopped onto the cabinets and skittered into the vent, which shown a bouncing orange and the sound of its tiny feet scratching the metal ventilation ducts was dwarfed only by the screams of all of them.

Thrashing on the ground, eye leaking into his hand, Manny convulsed one final time before losing consciousness. He could not feel Gale's arm loop under his own or the pull of her weak legs yanking him out of the burning room. As she dragged him through the doorway, she watched the smoke bellow from the vents and roil off the mounds of paper and crinkled walls. Outside, she sat next to her son as the neighbors filed out of their homes, careful not to cross the safe threshold of the street, and the sound of a fire engine whirred in the distance. She said nothing, only watched the flames flare out of the melting windows and out like hair from the tattered shingles, the sounds of her belabored breathing oddly apish.

—ETC.—

Tonight We Dine on Literature

Maxwell Worthington ran into his small house and bolted for the rotary phone. He flicked the numbers with stubby fingers and struggled to catch his breath. The phone rang endlessly. He undid his blue bowtie and gulped at the cool air. Someone picked up the line, and he gripped the table the phone was set on. "Mother, thank God! I've just been assailed by some... some *creature*. I can't even describe it, but it was filthy and horrid and it hissed at me! In the library. I saw it on the fourth floor! Oh, God, it was horrible. It came at me like a dog or a giant rat-man-thing! And before you say it, I am not drunk—I had too much champagne once, and you'll never let me live it down! But, it was there. I saw it and smelled it and some of its saliva is on my vest, the one you knit for me! It had claws and red eyes and it hissed at me, Mother. I need you to call the police. I know, I know, I could have done that, but these...yokels would think I'm mad. But, I'm not! It was there!"

He gasped and waited for his mother to respond. He nervously twirled the waxed ends of his moustache. A strange voice answered. "Muthafucka, you call this numba again, I'ma go over there and whup yo' dumb monkey ass," it said and hung up.

The next day, he found Manuel behind the library smoking a thin joint of skunky weed. His gray jumpsuit was dirty and reminded Maxwell of his dreams and that thing. The tattered robes. The long neck. The naked tail. "Manuel!" Maxwell barked, and the worker inhaled sharply and coughed. He dropped the joint into the grass and began to explain, but Maxwell waved his jittery words away. "Never mind that, Manuel," he said, pronouncing the name 'man-well.' "I need you to come with me to the fourth floor immediately. There is some kind of...animal up there. Do you have any sort of bludgeoning implements in your supply shed?"

109

"Any what?" Manuel said and squinted at the man. He wasn't high yet, but the fat librarian spoke so strangely it was hard to follow him. Maxwell stood in the ankle high grass wearing his pressed khaki's, robin's egg blue sweater-vest, and yellow bowtie. He nervously crinkled the edges of his moustache.

Maxwell sighed and shook his head, "Something to, as you would say, bash his expletive brains in. A stick or a hammer. Anything?"

Manuel shrugged and motioned for Maxwell to follow him. The shed was behind the crumbling library in the shadow of a tall ash tree, and the inside was plastered with the faded clippings of men's magazines. Maxwell shuddered at the sight of the faded breasts and auto-machinery; Manuel went to a cork board where his tools hung. He found a hammer and a large wrench for the water pipes. "Mr. Maxwell," Manual told him. "What exactly did you see up there?"

"I'd rather not describe the wretched thing to you," Maxwell replied.

"That's all right. But, it'd help me get an idea of what I'm looking for."

"Oh, you'll know once you've seen the disgusting creature," Maxwell said and shivered, making his round belly shake from side to side.

Manual shrugged, and they went out of the shed. Two doves watched them from the tree and flew off when they slammed the rusty door shut behind them. Maxwell held the hammer by the end with two fingers as if it were a dormant snake. In the elevator, Maxwell's teeth chattered audibly. "You all right, Mr. Maxwell?" Manuel asked.

Maxwell gulped hard and gasped, "I'm fine. I'm fine. The beast just gave me quite a fright yesterday."

"Must've," Manuel agreed. "Lots of animals loose around here, though. I take it it wasn't the same in the city."

By blessed Jehovah, no. Only purebred dogs and pigeons," Maxwell said. "An occasional alley cat."

"Yeah, San Casimiro's a different story," Manuel chuckled. "One of the only places left where you can see a man water his horse the same place you gas up."

The doors opened and they stepped out cautiously. Manuel started to speak, but Maxwell silenced him, and the look in his colored eyes spoke of a great mission of stealth. He whispered, "I'll show you where I found it," and slowly walked through the dark floor. The big bay windows filtered in the morning light, and Manuel watched the dust motes kick up with Maxwell's creeping walk. Manuel looked out onto the town and tried to spot his house, but focused on the swaying green of the *monte* that surrounded San Casimiro except for the slick black cut of the highway. The wind shook the trees and the worker leaned forward to see them better, but Maxwell called for him.

He was at the far corner of the floor and Manuel went to him. Some of the books were thrown off the shelves and tattered as if eaten. Bits of paper, transparent with spittle, lay on the old carpet. "The Spenserian beast was here, see?" Maxwell said and pointed.

Manuel squatted down and examined the scene. He found tiny droppings and used the tip of his wrench to knock them around. "Mr. Maxwell," he chuckled. "Don't tell me you got spooked by some little mice. That's what got to these books. You can even see their little teeth marks. See?" he asked and pointed to the tiny tears on a discarded page.

"It was not a rat of any variety, common or otherwise!'" Maxwell shouted in the quiet floor. "It was the size of a large canine. I swear it on my honor," he said and put his fist over his heart.

"That just doesn't make any sense," Manuel told him. "How'd it get in here? Why didn't it tear this whole place up? Shit all over the floor?"

"I don't know, Manuel! I'm not experienced in detective work. Let alone animal detective work. I can't tell you the purpose of some wild dog or crazed man!" The large fellow looked at the scene and caught sight of a hair stuck between the metal slats of the shelves. He pulled it out delicately and presented it to Manuel. "If it doesn't make sense, *Manuel*, then how do you explain this? Does this look like it came off the ordinary, household rodent? Hmm? No, it doesn't. Something is up here, and we need to find it."

They searched the whole floor and found nothing save the high pitched chatter of mice in the walls, which Maxwell jumped at, ready to attack. "Mr. Maxwell," Manuel said and checked the clock on the wall. "It's getting to that time. We should open up. That hair probably came off of Leti. She's got one hell of a rat's nest on her head. She'll probably want that back," he said pointing at the hair. "*Brujas* don't like to leave anything of theirs behind." He left Maxwell to stare at the wiry fur in his hand and went out behind the library to try to find his joint.

Thirty minutes after Maxwell unlocked the decorative doors, the first of them trickled in. Children. A dozen of them. Stocky women with gnarled fingers, and the same dead eyes left them at the doorstep until after five o'clock. The first was Juan, a four year old whose nose continuously dripped, and then Maria, seven and hyperactive. Maxwell prayed that Rudolfo would not come, but at nine fifteen, like clockwork, he came in and hooted like an owl. Maxwell jumped and leaned over the counter, "What have I told you? Quiet!" he yelled, though he knew it was of no use.

Rudolfo had not always been that way. Once, when Maxwell had first moved to San Casimiro, he thought that Rudolfo was smart. He read quietly, asked questions in a respectful whisper. But, something had happened to him. The parents had tried to say something had happened there, in the library, but Maxwell dismissed it as nonsense from nonsensical people. The locals always seemed to blame everyone but themselves. The boy was now touched in the head and was left in Maxwell's care five days a week so that his parents could have moments of peace from his ramblings.

Most of the children slept, leaving Maxwell to his reading, but ever since the San Casimiro Public Library became synonymous with a federal funded daycare, he hadn't found a moment to himself. All around the first floor, he propped up mirrors to view every aisle in elongated clarity. One of the next things Maxwell had done was close off the third and fourth floors. Leti had told him the county wouldn't like him closing off anything to the public, but after three weeks, no one noticed. Besides, Maxwell had told her, he wouldn't want to find Rudolfo fiddling with himself at the sight of large breasted tribeswomen of god-knows-where. But, the boy kept himself occupied by flipping through an old picture book of Japanese ink-paintings.

Leti strolled in at ten. She smelt of Virginia Slims and black coffee. Even Rudolfo respectfully ceased his giggling until she was far away. Maxwell noticed their little brown faces avert when the plump woman went by and remembered what Manuel had said. She went behind the counter and greeted him before going into the break room to put away her things. Maxwell slid his embroidered book-mark into the page of his copy of Edith Wharton and followed her.

"Leti," he said. She didn't look at him. "Leti, I have a question for you. I hope it is not too personal or offensive, but I need to ask you. My life depends on it."

She turned and gave him a strange look. Adjusting her glasses on her short nose, she said, "Well, ask it then, Max. You don't have to be so formal all the time, you know?"

"Very well," he coughed and stood taller as if waiting for the hangman to flip the switch. "Rumor has it that you, um, are some sort of dabbler in the arcane arts. Is that true?"

"A what? Who called me that?" she blurted and scrunched her face.

"A witch."

"A witch! Who the—why would—Max, is this because you thought I was the one moving your bookmark around? I already told you, I didn't touch one yarn on that thing."

"No, no," he stammered and put out his hands. "No, it's just that, um, the other day, I heard that you were a practitioner of the black arts. And, strange as it may seem, it is imperative that I find out if there is any validity to such a claim. Is it true?"

Leti put her hand on her plump hip and balked at him. "No, Max, I am not a damn witch. I was really into The Cure in high school, and that rumor just took off. I swear. My aunt from New Mexico is a *curandera*, but that's it."

"I see," Maxwell said to himself and twirled at the end of his moustache. "Would there be any way that you could get her here? Soon?"

"You know what they pay me," she shot back. "I can barely afford a six-pack of Keystone on the weekends. And what do you think *she* makes? This isn't Mexico anymore. She comes once a year."

"What if I provided the necessary funding for such an endeavor?" Maxwell interrupted. "What if I pay her for the journey and a... consultation. Please, I'll pay for it all. I just need her to get here."

"Do you know what it costs to call New Mexico? There goes my six-pack."

"Call from here," he begged her. "The county will bear that burden. Please, won't you?"

"Fine," she sighed and rolled her eyes. "What do you need to ask her anyway. I don't have *the gift*, but I picked up this and that."

"There is something on the fourth—"

In the library, the sound of a dozen children rang out, vibrating the door with shouts and laughter and cries of disgust and more laughter.

Maxwell looked to the door and ran to it. "Get her here!" he shouted at Leti and stepped into the chaos. In the corner, Rudolfo sat atop one of the tables with an ink-painting strewn across it. He pumped himself furiously, drooling and hyperventilating. "Oh, my sweet heavenly Father!" Maxwell cried and took the boy by the shoulders. He pushed Rudolfo outside into the heat and called him a little savage. The boy went on as a few lonely cars crossed paths before the library.

Maxwell returned and told the rest to mind themselves and went to close the book Rudolfo had lusted over. The almost crude portrait of a geisha with a parasol looked up at him. Along with a stocky, pale thigh, a single breast was exposed. The nipple, a mere dab of the brush, was wet. He took the book by the corner and dumped it on his side of the counter. Another book to shut away in the upper floors. He looked up as though able to pierce through the bricks and mortar and saw into the top floor. A shudder went through him when he felt it look back.

The day was long and uneventful. The children flipped through the same picture books Maxwell left in their reach and occasionally drifted by his counter to ask one stupid question or the other about him. Why was he so tall? Why were his arms so thin and his belly so round? Why did he talk funny? Maxwell would give them long, annoyed lectures: "My God! Why is it you little ragamuffins can't seem to understand the idea of manners and tact? The very existence of the forms of society holds the fabric of this country together. You do not ask someone such inquiries. It is shameful. It would be the same as *me* asking *you* why you are so short or so stupid or so undeniably filthy. Now, be gone! Out of my sight! It is by my benevolent mercy alone that you are not out in the sun, baking and dancing by the highway."

The minutes ticked by and one by one, the children were taken. Each pair of dirty shoes that left was a weight lifted off his shoulders, until all that was left was a single boy asleep under a table. When he was gone, Maxwell breathed a sigh of relief. In the office, Leti listened to the radio. He leaned back in his chair for a moment and sprung up to his feet. He collected copies of Dr. Suess and *Peanut's Gang and the Great Pumpkin* and put them into a bin to sort out later.

Though he couldn't think of anyone going up to the second floor, he moved to the stairs. At first he hesitated, taking the first step as though he tread on a tiger's jaw. He grew bolder with each step, whispering to himself, "Last time, it was dusk. The horrible beast is probably afraid of the sun and all of its wondrous properties. Yes, I'm certain it scorches its demon skin."

The floor was silent and musty. The tables, vandalized with third rate carvings, wore a thin layer of dust. He moved through the rows, but found no evidence that anyone had been there in weeks. A noise startled him. "Leti?" he said after it. "Leti, was that you?" he asked again, though he knew the answer.

Silence.

Maxwell crept out of the aisles and looked up the stairs to the third floor. The sun cast deep shadows, and all he could make out were the silhouettes of bookshelves. A chitter kept him fixated on the spot, and something darted across his view. A rat. Another followed. And another. Tiny beings of shadow ran past, squeaking and testing the air with their noses. In the midst of them, it came.

It moved on all fours, neck strained and downward. The tattered clothes it wore hung like strips of flesh, and its tail swished sickly in the air. It stopped and sniffed the air in gulps, settling on Maxwell's direction. Their eyes met. A scared blue and a glowing red. "*Yo te conozco,*" it hissed and drug its claws across the steps, hunching like a gargoyle. "*Eres el tonto. Tu no sabes nada importante. Y yo quiero sabiduria.*" Its laugh nearly sent Maxwell to the floor. "*Vete y no regreses o te mato. Entiendes, tonto?*"

Maxwell couldn't move.

"*Andale tonto!*" it raged and lunged forward.

Maxwell ran to the stairs, nearly tumbling onto the first floor. "Leti!" he screamed. "Oh, my God! Leti!" He burst into the office to find her tapping her fingernails to the tune of some obnoxious corrido. "Don't tell me you didn't hear any of that."

"What?" she asked and turned down the radio. "What did you say?"

Maxwell snarled to himself and took a deep breath. "I said, don't tell me you didn't hear that."

"Hear what?"

"Some foul abomination," he roared and pointed to the ceiling. "The same abomination that accosted me yesterday. It spoke to me! Leti, have you called your aunt yet?"

"No," she answered flatly. She waited for Maxwell to say something, but he didn't. "Oh, you wanted me to do that today?"

"Yes!"

"But, I don't have anywhere to put her."

"If it will get her here sooner," Maxwell said, flustered. "I will let her lodge with me! I don't care if that means I have to sleep outside, just get her here!"

"Who knows how many days she'll want to stay? Maybe three, if she's free," Leti said and smiled. "Hey, that rhymed."

"Heaven help me," Maxwell gasped. "Fine. I'll be taking a leave of absence until then. Call me when she arrives."

"Why are you taking time off?"

"Until this…this creature is dealt with, I won't spend another moment in this murderous place," he ranted and went out the door.

"Sounds good to me," Leti said to herself and turned the radio up.

He spent the three days pouring over old books of myths, but his selection was limited to any books he carted from the city and whatever was available at work. There was nothing about giant-talking rats that haunted libraries. Not in the stories of the Greeks or the Romans. The detailed studies of local Indian tribes proved to be equally as pointless. The closest he came to it was in a collection of works by Milton. The play was called "Comus" and in it, the spawn of a goddess and sprite turned men to beasts with a magical elixir, but he doubted this had anything to do with the man-rat.

On the third day, he woke to a loud pounding on his door. He threw on a periwinkle robe and answered it. He smelt her before he saw her. The noxious mix of sweat and soil and Zest soap and cheap cigarettes. She was short with a face of tanned leather. She puffed her rolled cigarette and asked if she could come in. He gave a gracious bow and motioned for her to come inside. Before entering, she touched a small pouch that nestled between her breasts and muttered something to the entrance.

Her burlap sack of belongings was dropped beside the coat rack, and she stood examining the living room with her cigarette drizzling ash onto the carpet. At the sight of an ornate Celtic cross, she scoffed.

"I'm sorry, Miss…"

"My name is not important," she grumbled. "Too many know it as it is."

"Well, then, Miss, must you smoke in here? My sinuses have a particular aversion to the acrid nature of dried tobacco smoke."

The old witch glared at him. "Yes," she barked. "Yes, it is necessary. The herbs in this cigarette will allow me to identify the spirits, though they may not want to be seen."

"Yes, yes," Maxwell stuttered. "I understand, but the spirit in question isn't located here in my home. I'm sure Leti told you as much."

"Leticia told me nothing," the witch said. "She told me to come quickly, and that was all. In truth, I felt foolish rushing over here. I had much work to do against another *bruja* in New Mexico. But, such is the way of family."

"Well, would you like to visit the site in question?" Maxwell asked sheepishly.

"No," the *bruja* said. "That is tomorrow's work. Now," she balked and went into the kitchen. "What do you have for an old woman to eat?"

Maxwell looked at her dusty bag of possessions, noting the grime on it, and wondered how long he could stand his houseguest, *bruja* or not.

Maxwell felt foolish, standing in the middle of the library behind the old witch as if her stocky frame could hide or protect him. He'd closed the place—under the guise of reshelving—and brought the old woman in the morning. Even in the middle of the first floor, the old witch took out a rolled cigarette and lit it. The smoke was thick and white and seemed to cling to her and follow her around the room. She absently took long pulls off the cigarette and blew plumes of the smoke at the corners of the room. She read the twists of the smoke in the air before moving on.

The old witch did this through the break room, the front desk, beneath the tables, and into the chairs. Maxwell watched in a vexed pose, knowing full well he'd never be able to get the smell of her cheap cigarettes out of the place. Knowing that, he thought of how badly his house would smell after the old witch left.

"There is nothing on this floor," the old witch said and turned to Maxwell.

"I know that," Maxwell told her. "As I said over breakfast, the creature is in the upper floors. I suppose that the sun coming in through the front door may have some adverse effect for it."

"You are a stupid man," the old witch said.

"What! How dare you—"

"There are many demons that walk freely in the light," the old witch said and went to the second floor.

The *bruja* stopped at the entrance to the second floor, keeping her feet on the final step. With her stubby fingers, she touched the place where the creature had been and closed her eyes as if reading the miasma of the place they stood. "Ah," she said. "*Un puente.*"

"Excuse me," Maxwell asked, coming up behind her like a blubbering man-child. "Did you find something? What are we dealing with?"

"No, foolish man," the old witch said. "How could I know what *I* am dealing with without seeing it? If anything, I have found a reason why it may have come here." She retrieved a candle from her bag and prayed over it. She lit it with a long, rose colored match. "You are not from this land, yes?"

"No," Maxwell admitted. "I'm from the Dallas metroplex, respectively."

"Yes," the old witch said and went further inside, careful to keep the fragrant candle before her. "That explains much. San Casimiro, for more years than I have walked this earth, has been a strange place. The people here keep their mouths quiet about it. But, even before this was Texas, when this was simply land, things have occurred here. Monstrous things. Beasts come here that should not be here. People are here that should not be, yourself included. The rules of the world do not hold true in this place. Years ago, there was a man found here that had lived beyond death. A woman gave birth to snakes. And the last time I came to this wretched place, I saw a being so fearsome, I could do nothing but hide from it."

"But, why?" Maxwell asked. "Why here?"

"It is like I said," the old witch told him. "This place is a *puente*, a bridge. Others exist, though I have only heard of them from my mother and her mother before her. They are places where the reality of this world and the reality of the other collide. The horrid creatures that live in the world beyond this one gain entry into our world through bridges like San Casimiro."

"How do we...shut these...bridges down, may I ask?" Maxwell said. "Do you know some sort of spell—"

Before he could finish the statement, the old witch spun and slapped him. She glared at him for a moment and spit on the ground. "Do not speak to me as though I am some magician or sorcerer. My magic is a God-fearing magic."

"I am sorry," Maxwell said, holding his face, unsure of what to do. He hadn't been slapped since he was in grade school, though it was also by an old woman.

"As you should be," the old witch said as she continued down the book-filled lanes. "But, to answer your foolish question, there is nothing we can do to stop it. A bridge is a link from one world to another. They were formed before time was time. Before mankind was able to venture from their caves. That kind of connection is much too strong to destroy utterly. But, I believe, I will be able to stop it for a moment."

"What good will that do?"

The second slap was louder and much more painful. "Idiot. When I speak of moments, I do not mean *our* moments. I speak of a cosmic moment. A moment for God. That, *tonto*, is longer than you will live. To stop it for an instant is to say that you will never see this creature, whatever it is, again."

"What does that mean?"

"Not to see something?"

"No," Maxwell said, holding his cheek. "That word, tone-toe. What does it mean?

"It means idiot," the witch said, her tone showing her aggravation with having to be followed by such a man. "Why do you ask such a foolish question?"

"Because...that thing...it called me that."

The old witch's eyes widened. "It spoke to you?" she gasped. "And it spoke in a human tongue?"

"Yes," Maxwell said. "I suppose, I have not fully developed a grasp on the language."

"You must tell me what it told you," the old witch said frantically. Maxwell tried as best he could to mimic the sounds, the shape of the words. She corrected him and substituted sounds for others to see if there was any clarity to be gained. Once he was finished, the old witch stood and thought. "The creature said that you knew nothing. That you were a fool. It has come for wisdom, it said. Also, it said if you came back, it would kill you. But, that is not the worst part."

"How is *that* not the worst part!" Maxwell shouted and winced as he did. Not only had he shouted in his own library, but he shouted in a library that was inhabited by some thing from another world, a world that, compared to his, was infinite and terrible.

"It said that it knew you," the old witch said. "We would do well to stay away from here."

"Why? How does that creature knowing me matter?"

"Because these things do not like to be seen more than once," she said. "If you stay here, you will die. And, if I stay here, slowed down by an idiot like yourself, I will have all my knowledge taken from me. Though that is not so fearful for you, my wisdom is what sustains me. For now, we must move forward. Once we find where it hides, my task will be much easier."

Together, the old witch and Maxwell went to the third floor. Again, she stopped on the threshold, but not to touch the border of it. She lifted her candle and spoke in a tongue that Maxwell could not understand. "Come out," she bellowed. She fished a cigarette from her pocket and lit it with the candle. "Come and face me, devil. I do not fear you."

"*Entonces, tu eres más tonta que el gordo, pinche bruja,*" Maxwell heard. "*Vete, vieja fea. Déjame comer en paz.*"

"I will not go," the old witch said.

The creature smiled at her, revealing sharp lower fangs of iron. It narrowed its red eyes and pointed at her and Maxwell. "*Vete de aqui,*" the creature said.

The walls vibrated, and the shelves shook. It retreated further into the darkness, but a sound surrounded them. The sound of soft bodies hitting the carpeted floor. A chittering of a thousand tiny mouths. Soon, they came into the small ring of light around them. The rats. So thick and numerous, they blotted out the carpet's design and left trails of devoured fibers and pellet shaped feces as they passed like a horde of locusts in some Biblical smiting. The old witch looked confident and blew a lungful of smoke at the charging rodents. They barreled through the smoke and climbed onto her. She fell back onto Maxwell, and together they tumbled down the stairs.

When Maxwell had his bearings regained, he realized, his face had landed directly between the old witch's legs. The smell was ferocious. The rats cascaded over them, nipping at their skin with tiny teeth and scratching at their eyes and hair with their small claws. Maxwell slapped at them without thinking, without caring how many times he hit the rude *bruja*. She tried to find her feet, but Maxwell's flopping in the sea of rats caught her legs and she collapsed, crushing a dozen of the mad rodents with her girth. The old witch used Maxwell's body to stand and delivered a kick with her stubby legs before retreating completely, leaving Maxwell to deal with the rats that threatened to devour him.

They attacked his lips and eyes, and were it not for his thick glasses, the tiny beasts would have blinded him. But, he rose from them like a primordial god, though screaming as if a terrorized women in a drive-in horror film, waving his arms, sending the small creatures to crash against the walls and shelves. Blindly, he ran towards the stairs, crushing tiny bodies in his wake, and tumbled down into the first floor, coated in the crushed hides of the rats that still followed him, until Maxwell was out of the door.

Outside, he nearly fell over the old witch again. She stood there, wiping the flecks of gore and bits of fur off of her. They did not speak immediately, still scared and inspecting themselves. Both of their faces were a collection of red cuts with thin lines of blood dried to their cheeks. Their lips were open from being nibbled on and bits of their scalp showed through the clumps of hair that had been eaten from their heads.

"What was that!" he yelled at her. "I was under the notion that you were some powerful sorceress, but here I am, riddled with bites, tetanus coursing through my shaken veins. What sideshow shenanigans are you trying to pull?"

"Be quiet, idiot," the old witch said. "I did not foresee—"

"I should say that you did not!" Maxwell fumed. Cars on the highway were slowing to watch the spectacle: a large man dressed in pastels berating an old Mexican woman, who moved to slap him. "Had you seen that happening, I imagine you would have done more than attempt to give them a mix of cancer and heart disease."

"I will not stand for such insolence," the old witch said. "I am the most respected and powerful *curandera* in all of New Mexico!"

"Well, you smelly old harridan, you are not in New Mexico!" he yelled back. "You are in Texas, and apparently, whatever voodoo you propose to practice has shown to be useless! I'm surprised that I didn't break my neck falling down that stairwell."

"I will do nothing more for you or your problem, you gigantic oaf," the old witch said.

"Like you have done anything at all, except tell me a colorful story about unsubstantiated folklore!" Maxwell dared.

"Do not push me," the old witch warned. "Another word from you, and I will not hesitate to put a curse on you so foul it will make your seed smell like cow dung. It will make every waking breath you take taste of death."

"Go, then," Maxwell said. "You have my money. You have your ticket home. Go. Leave and be useless somewhere else."

The old witch narrowed her eyes and made small motions with her hands. She rambled quickly in a tongue that Maxwell knew nothing of, and once she was done, she flicked her fingers at him three times and spat on the ground between them. "To hell with you, Maxwell Worthington. May your foolishness make you burn." Maxwell was visibly afraid of the witch's motion and her guttural talk, so he did not follow her when she walked away from the library, an unfiltered cigarette, a holy cigarette, burning between her teeth.

For two days, Maxwell waited for the curse to take effect. But, as far as he could tell, his seed didn't smell any different and neither did his breath.

He took to pouring over more and more books about folklore, trying to find something that would describe the man-rat, reveal why it haunted Maxwell's place of employment. There was nothing. All he could find was some obscure passage that said, demons and spirits, regardless of type or origin, must have a place, a site to inhabit. If the site was destroyed, purged as the book said, the spirit would wander until it found some other place to haunt or simply die from a sort of spiritual starvation. Maxwell read this, took a sheet of paper, and copied the information. He had always detested marking up a book, desperate situation or not.

The second night, the phone rang. The loud ringer startled Maxwell and made him answer the phone a little out of breath. "Yes?" he said.

"Maxwell!" a shrill voice pealed. "Maxwell, my dear boy, where have you been!"

"Mother," Maxwell said and sighed. "I have been rather preoccupied as of late."

"That is no excuse, Maxwell, to neglect your poor mother," his mother told him. "I have been worried sick these last few days. Why, it is quite unlike you to not call in such a long time. I had thought you dead or worse."

"Well, mother," Maxwell said. "I would say that I am much, much worse than that."

"How dreadful!" his mother shrieked. "I knew you should never have taken that dreadful position in the middle of nowhere. All those stories about South Texas are hardly what I would have called appetizing. What have those back-wood savages done to you, my poor child!"

"Mother, they have done nothing," Maxwell said. "But, there is a type of…how should I say this delicately…"

"Do not say it delicately, dear boy," his mother said. "Tell it to me bluntly, but with softness."

"Mother," Maxwell said. "As the sole keeper of this foul bit of knowledge, I am aware of how it must sound to another. If I put it bluntly, to be blunt, you would think I was mad or worse."

"Maxwell," she told him. "By you continuing to bounce around the proverbial bush, I do think you mad."

"Very well," Maxwell said and steadied himself. "Mother, about a week ago, I was in the library. It was a very ungodly hour, but I had been called over since I had forgotten that scarf you'd knit—"

"Maxwell! Please do not use contractions," his mother told him. "They are dreadfully vulgar."

"Please, mother," Maxwell bade her. "I was in the library and heard a noise come from the top floor of the building. I foolishly went up to inspect it and—"

"Oh, lord!" his mother shrieked. "Were they burglars?"

"No, mother, it was—"

"Please, God, do not tell me you were held against your will and molested!"

"Heavens, no!" Maxwell shouted.

"Do not yell at me, Maxwell," his mother said. "I cannot be yelled at in my current state. Your slow story is positively horrid on my imagination. You have yet to tell me what was there, and already I have imagined at least seven or eight crimes of both violent and sexual natures that could have been inflicted upon you."

"Mother, I assure, I was not poked, prodded, molested, or anything of the sort," Maxwell said. "I…when I was on the fourth floor, I followed the sound and I saw…a creature."

"What kind of creature? Oh, Maxwell, you were not attacked were you?"

"Only verbally and visually," Maxwell said.

"What? Verbally?"

"Yes, mother. This creature…it spoke to me."

"Do not be foolish, Maxwell," his mother said. "If it were a creature, it would not have been able to accost you at all."

"Mother," Maxwell said. "It was not all creature, and it was not all man. It was some strange perversion of both. It looked like a rat mixed with a man. But, right as you called, I think I found the solution. According to my books, a demon needs a place to call home else—"

"Maxwell," his mother giggled. "Did you say *demon*? I hope living in that little hovel of a town has not made you take to hard cider again. You are always so dreadfully ghastly when you have consumed too much hard cider."

"Mother!"

"Do not yell at me, Maxwell. I will not stand for it."

"I was not, have not, and will not be drunk," Maxwell said calmly. "I know what I have seen. Two days ago, I employed a witch of sorts—well, what these South Texans see as a witch—and we were attacked by the creature once again. It seems that only one thing can be done, and I intend on doing it."

"Oh, and what is that Maxwell?"

"I intend to fully and completely destroy the library of San Casimiro," Maxwell said. Once his mother asked him if he was drunk again, he hung up.

Maxwell walked into the one filling station; he was smiling beneath his moustache. The sight unnerved most of the people he passed—the one old woman gassing up her single-cab truck and young rancher watering his spotted horse—but, Maxwell didn't care. He knew the secret. True, the books he'd found said nothing of that specific entity or how to deal with it. But, he felt as though it would work. All creatures needed a place to hide, to escape the turmoil of the world outside. His own was a small, one bedroom house a few blocks away; the man-rat, its roost was in the library, comfortably hidden in the shadows of the aisles.

He purchased two gallon canisters, a lighter, and a copy of the *San Casimiro Howler*. He paid the clerk and asked him to put a few dollars on one of the pumps. "If there is some I don't use," he told the acne ridden kid, "you are very welcome to keep the change." The kid made no answer, only wrapped the register a few times and told him that pump two was open. Maxwell went to it with long strides, the smile still there. He filled the first canister, but only filled the other half way before his money ran out. He took them both to the front of the library and looked over his shoulders; there was nothing there save for a speeding car blasting north on the black highway.

Maxwell opened the door and slipped inside. He went to the children's books and magazines and tore the pages from them, throwing them like confetti over his head as though he was the mad conductor of a procession of the insane. He flung the covers to the walls and turned over the tables, kicking at the legs and flinging the broken pieces at random. The sunlight was waning. It cast an odd shadow, deep and twisted, behind Maxwell. "Call me a fool, will you," Maxwell said. "I'm an idiot am I? Well, you foul rodent from hell, son of a bottom feeder and a ghostly whore, I learned your secret." He emptied the full canister of gasoline on the ground, dousing the piles of pages until they were translucent.

He went upstairs and threw more pages in a trail all around the room. With some effort, he tipped one of the shelves, sending it domino-like into the rest, which fell over with a crash, scattering books and scraps of garbage left by the few patrons San Casimiro afforded. He spilt some of the gasoline on the shelves and carpet. "Come on out, you rat," Maxwell said and threw the canister away. He looked up into the third floor, his newspaper and lighter at the ready. "Come out here, so I can murder you, abomination!"

There was a hissing laughter, and two red eyes blinked to life from the darkness. "*Que quieres, gran idiota?*" It crawled, dragging its tattered robes along the ground. Its naked tail whipped in the air, and the sound of its iron claws on the stairs was enough to make Maxwell shiver. "*Tienes frio, panzon?*" it giggled.

Maxwell lit the lighter and held it in front of him like a ward. "Say whatever you like in your demon speech," he said. "I know your secret now. And to think that you called me an idiot. Ha! Devil, witness your own demise. Fire came down from heaven and consumed the burnt offering and sacrifices, and the glory of the Lord filled the temple!" Maxwell yelled and lit some of the newspaper. He threw it and ran to the stairs. The whoosh of the fire consuming the musty old books and dried out fibers of the carpet was deafening. A screeching howl filled the second floor, but gave way to a cackling laughter. "I will not be detoured!" Maxwell swore and set the first floor ablaze.

He stood at the door and watched the stairwell. He wanted to see it fall and twist and writhe in pain, but the heat became too much for him. His nostrils were burning, and his eyes were horribly dry from the blaze he set. As he backed away, moving round the building to afford a more secret path home, the third floor had caught. Thick plumes of black smoke rolled out of the windows that burst from the heat. The fires bit at the rush of air as the dog a pilfered scrap. Under the branches of an ash tree, he watched the San Casimiro County Library burn.

It took forty minutes for any firefighter to come. They'd been at some strange eruption of poisonous gas a few miles from town, and many of them took ill from the thick purple cloud. They sprayed the outer walls of the library and into the windows for a few minutes before the building shuddered like an old cat and fell. A thick cloud of dust and ash squeezed out of it, enveloping the firefighters and a few cars on the highway.

Maxwell watched from further down the street, slowly and nonchalantly backtracked to his own home. As the firefighters dusted themselves off, Maxwell worried about what they might find. Soon, his worries subsided. The fire had gone on for a long time; the canisters of gasoline would have been burnt up, or any evidence of him handling them anyway. The store clerk could only say that Maxwell had bought gasoline and two canisters. And the lighter. But, all of those things were legal, Maxwell reminded himself. Who was to say that his car hadn't run out of gas, and he just needed a little to get home? Yes, Maxwell said to himself, he'd done nothing suspicious, even if it was his place of employment smoldering and sending up embers to the wind.

He went into his home, relieved to be out of the smoky air and into the smell of books and carpeting. When he looked into the living room, Maxwell dropped his keys and stood still. It was there, hunched over one of his older volumes of Lady Murosaki's works. At the sound of the keys, the creature shoved a few pages into its fanged mouth and turned; bits of shredded paper stuck out from between its lips. *"Hola, marrano. Te vez sorprendido."*

—ETC.—

About the Author

Mario E. Martinez founded San Casimiro, Texas in 2008 and quickly set to filling it with the exiled monsters and deranged fools of his overactive imagination. He currently teaches English at his hometown university in South Texas, where he lives. *San Casimiro, Texas: Short Stories* is his first collection.